# what's inside?

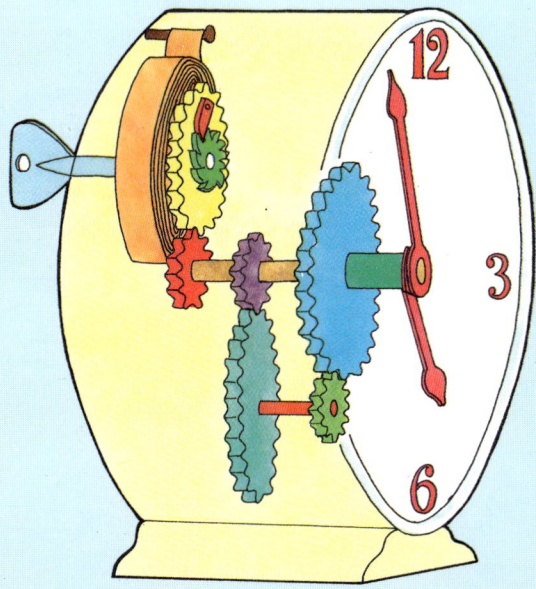

Margaret Crush

# what's inside?

**Illustrated by
Colin and Moira Maclean**

DRAGON BOOKS
Granada Publishing

Published by Dragon Hardbacks 1984
Granada Publishing Ltd
8 Grafton Street
London W1X 3LA

Copyright © Margaret Crush
Illustrations © Colin and Moira Maclean

British Library Cataloguing in Publication
Data
Crush, Margaret
  What's inside.
  1. Technology – Dictionaries, Juvenile
  I. Title
  603'.21      T9
  ISBN 0-246-11800-8

Printed in Spain by
Graficas Reunidas, Madrid

# what's inside?

What's down that hole? What's in an egg? What's in my leg? What's in a hoover, or a spray can, or a chocolate factory? What's inside?

Everyone wants to know, and being told is often not enough: they want to *look*.

Children can look inside all kinds of things in this book, from ants' nests to airports, and from the human body to building sites. Adults or older children can use the index to help find where the pictures are. There is plenty for you to talk about, and quiz questions at the end.

What's inside? is a book that will enable curious children (with their parents) to look inside places it's not always easy or safe to go into, and objects you can't always take apart. It also explains how, why and when things happen 'inside'.

There's lots to do too. When you've seen what's inside them and how they work, it's fun to make a model telephone or lift that works, or to watch ants make a nest in a jam jar. This book is for you to enjoy.

# Contents

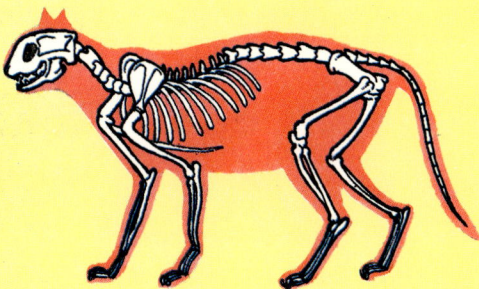

# A Tree

Lots of creatures live in trees. Animals eat the fruit, build nests and enjoy the shade.

butterfly

The leaves make food for the tree with water and sunlight.

squirrel

Flowers and then fruit grow on the branches.

magpie

chaffinch

moth

This is an apple tree

Apples are often made rotten by a little grub.

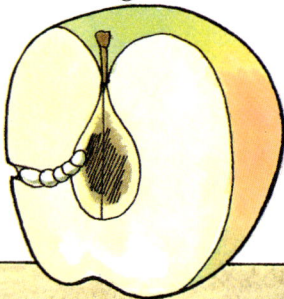

Bark protects the trunk.

The woodmouse nests in tree roots

The sap carries food and water up the tree trunk.

Roots suck up water from the ground.

A bee takes pollen to a flower. Now the flower can make a fruit.

The flowers turn into apples.
Inside these are pips.
These are seeds.
New trees will grow from them.

core

pip

apple

**Inside the trunk**
Every year a tree makes a new ring of wood. This is how it grows fatter. Count the rings of a cut-down tree to find out how old it was. One ring means one year, so ten rings are ten years.

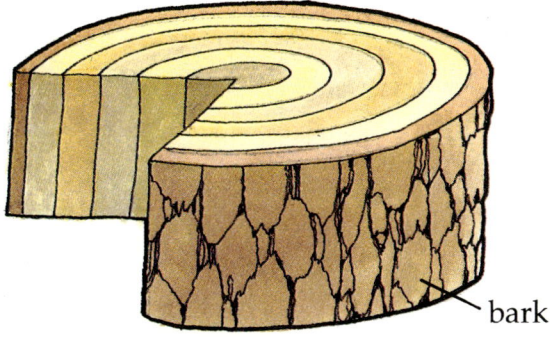

bark

How old was this tree?

**Grow an apple tree**

1 Plant some apple pips in some earth or compost.

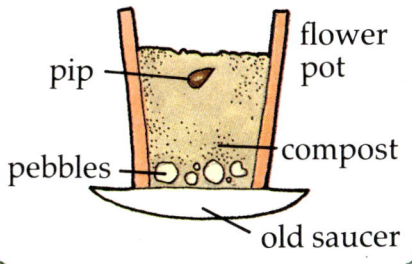

pip

flower pot

pebbles

compost

old saucer

2 Cover the pot with a piece of clear plastic.

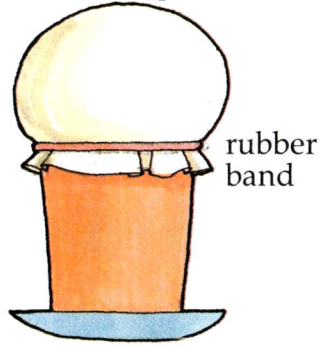

rubber band

Put it in a sunny place.

3 When tiny leaves pop up, take away the plastic.

Water the tiny plant once or twice a week.

4 When the little tree is bigger, plant it in the ground.

When you are grown up, you may even eat apples from it.

# An Ants' Nest

Ants build their nests under the ground. They make many rooms and tunnels. Each worker ant does a special job.

Winged ants (males and queens) go off to make new nests.

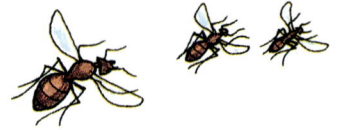

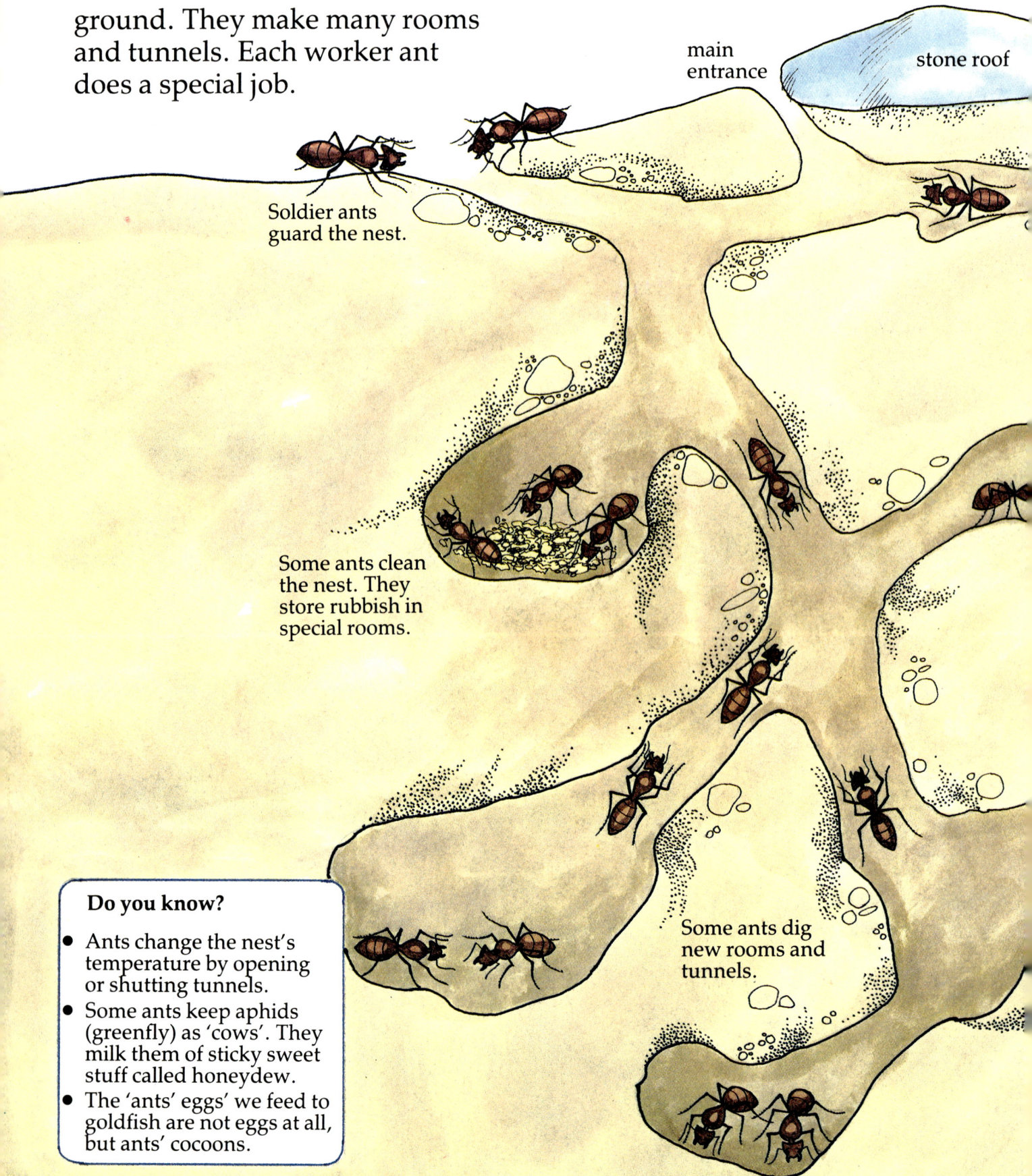

main entrance

stone roof

Soldier ants guard the nest.

Some ants clean the nest. They store rubbish in special rooms.

Some ants dig new rooms and tunnels.

**Do you know?**

- Ants change the nest's temperature by opening or shutting tunnels.
- Some ants keep aphids (greenfly) as 'cows'. They milk them of sticky sweet stuff called honeydew.
- The 'ants' eggs' we feed to goldfish are not eggs at all, but ants' cocoons.

Some worker ants collect food.

Ants eat food such as fruit, honey, grain or dead insects.

**Watch your own ants at work**

Make a nest like this with two jars. Put fine soil between them, and a few ants. Put food on the lid of the inner jar. The ants will tunnel through the soil to get the food.

Keep the nest in the dark for a few days.

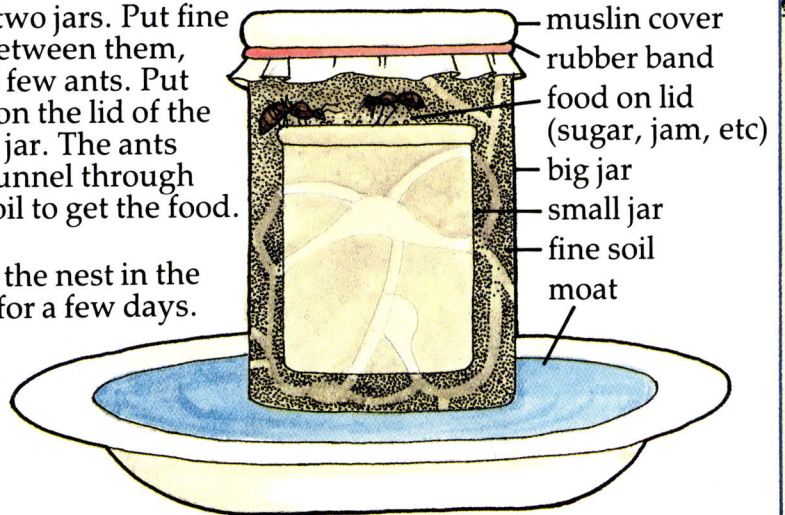

muslin cover
rubber band
food on lid (sugar, jam, etc)
big jar
small jar
fine soil
moat

Water with washing up liquid in it will stop the ants escaping.

grubs (larvae)

4 The grubs turn into pupae, each wrapped in its own cocoon.

3 Grubs which hatch from the eggs live in a special room.

cocoons

5 New young ants hatch from the pupae.

eggs

2 Worker ants carry the eggs to other rooms.

Male ants do no work at all. They just mate with the queen.

queen

1 Deep inside the nest the queen ant lays lots of eggs.

11

# A Beehive

Honey-bees live together in the wild. People also keep honey-bees in hives. Every nest has worker bees, male bees called drones, and a queen bee.

**Queen Bee**
The queen bee lays thousands of eggs a day.

**Worker bee**
Some worker bees collect food in pollen sacs. Some look after eggs and bee grubs. Some make new cells for the honeycomb, and some guard the hive.

**Drone**
Male bees do no work at all.

This bee is gathering nectar and pollen from a flower.

pollen sac

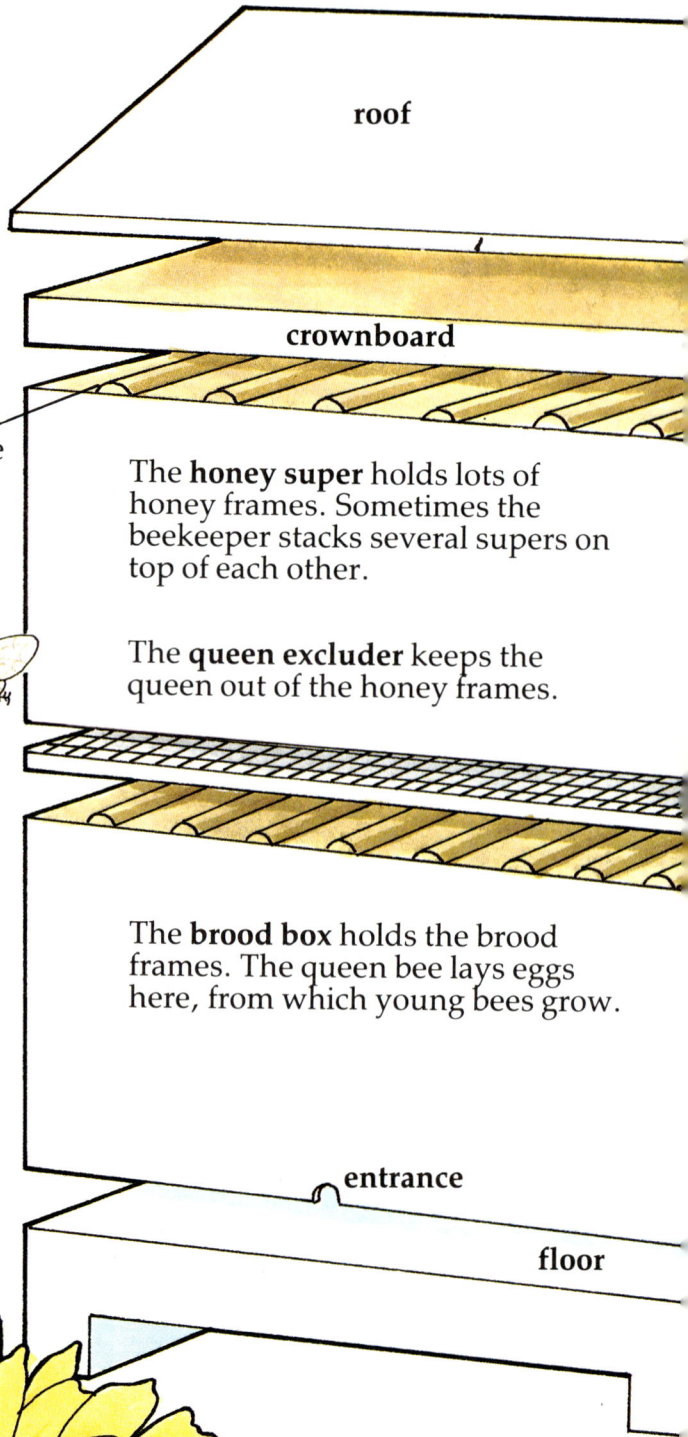

roof

crownboard

top of a frame

The **honey super** holds lots of honey frames. Sometimes the beekeeper stacks several supers on top of each other.

The **queen excluder** keeps the queen out of the honey frames.

The **brood box** holds the brood frames. The queen bee lays eggs here, from which young bees grow.

entrance

floor

A hive is a pile of boxes without tops or bottoms. Inside each box there are upright frames. The bees make honeycombs on these frames.

This is what a honeycomb looks like. In a real hive there would be only honey cells in the honey frame, and eggs, grubs and young bees in the brood frames.

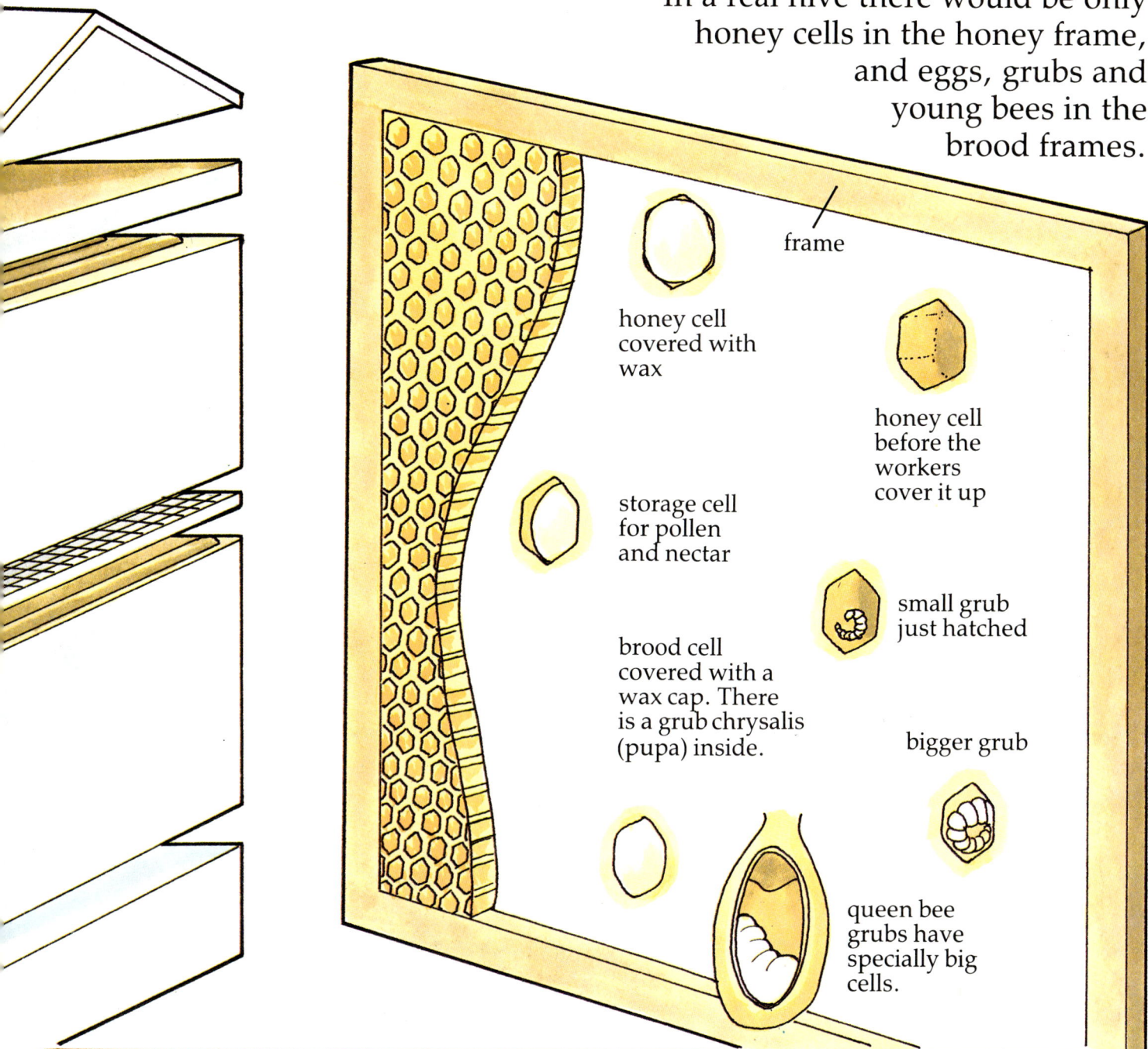

frame

honey cell covered with wax

honey cell before the workers cover it up

storage cell for pollen and nectar

small grub just hatched

brood cell covered with a wax cap. There is a grub chrysalis (pupa) inside.

bigger grub

queen bee grubs have specially big cells.

**How a young bee grows**

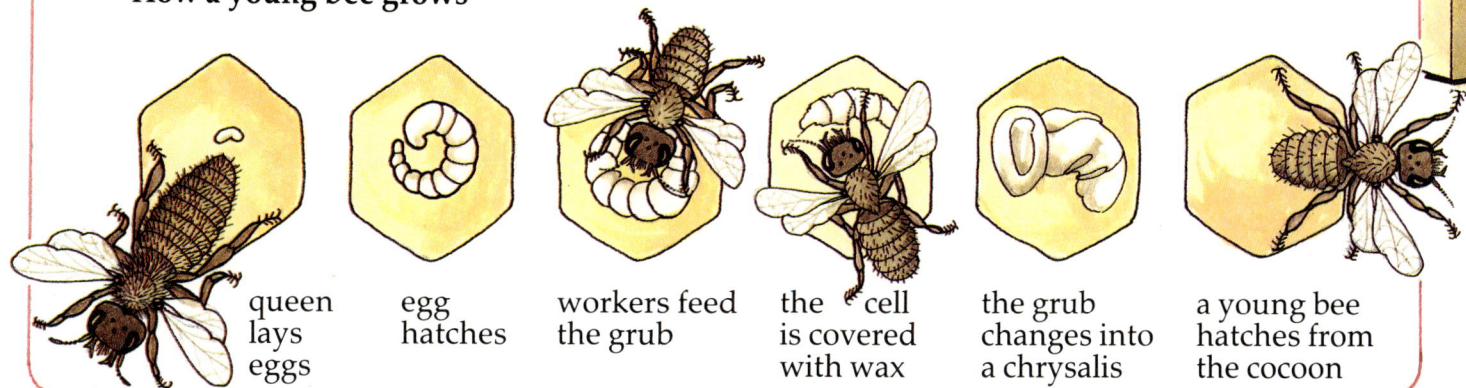

queen lays eggs

egg hatches

workers feed the grub

the cell is covered with wax

the grub changes into a chrysalis

a young bee hatches from the cocoon

# A Badger's Set

Badgers live in underground homes called sets. A set may be fifty or even a hundred years old.

front door

A badger's tunnels are sometimes two metres deep, and ten metres long.

old nursery

nursery

bracken bedding

## More about badgers

Badgers only come out at night. They sleep below ground during the day.

Badgers are very strong. They dig new tunnels with their big claws and teeth.

Badgers are very clean.

They take their bedding outside to air.

air shaft

pile of earth
and old bedding

back
door

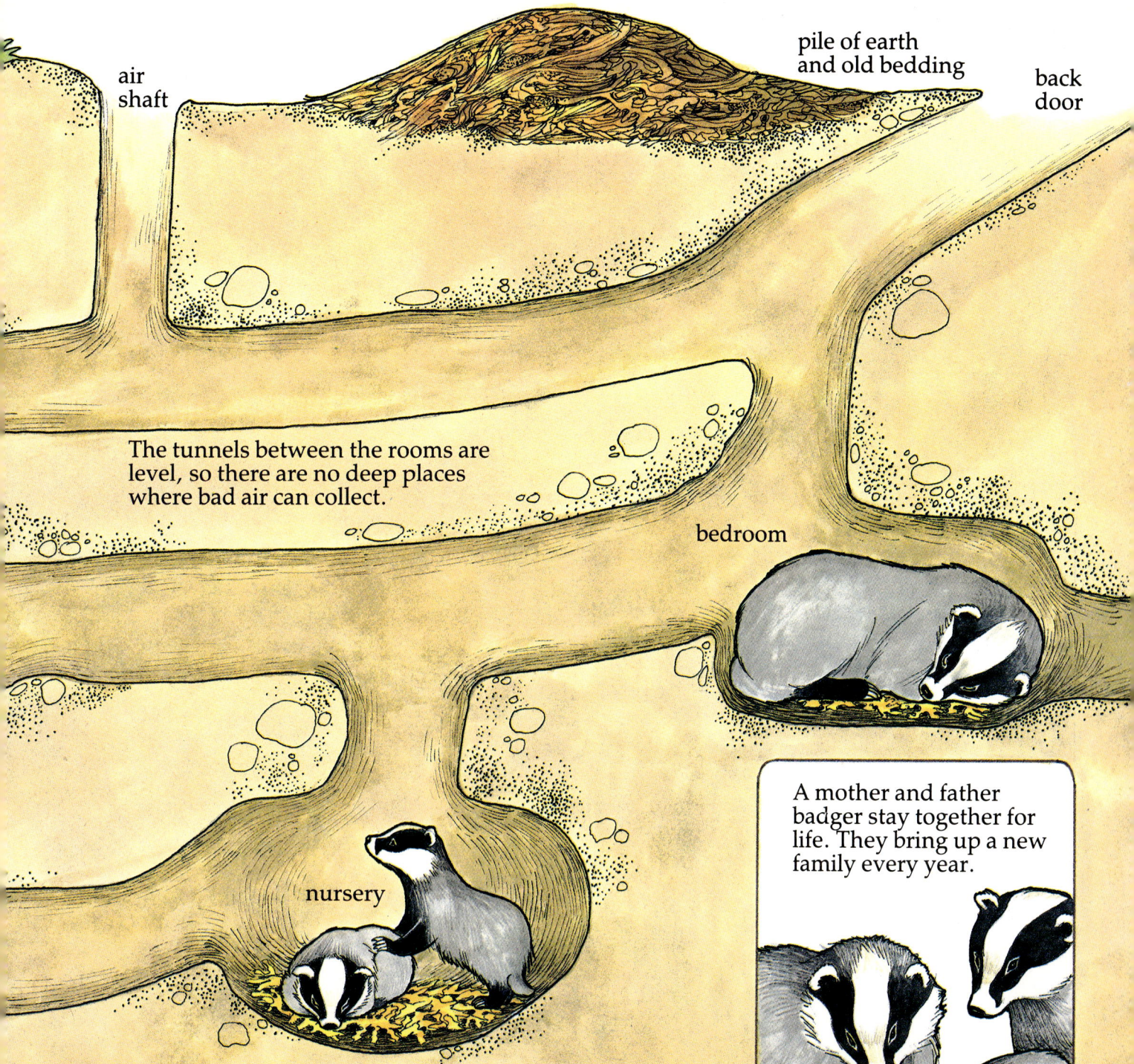

The tunnels between the rooms are
level, so there are no deep places
where bad air can collect.

bedroom

A mother and father
badger stay together for
life. They bring up a new
family every year.

nursery

worms

beetles

insects

caterpillars

fruit

bulbs

toadstools

Badgers dig lavatories
outside – away from their
set.

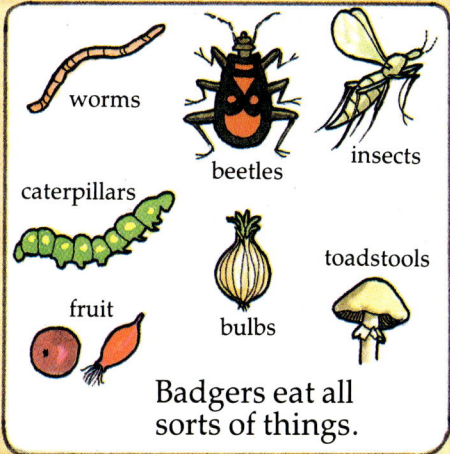

Badgers eat all
sorts of things.

Young badgers enjoy
playing games such as
king of the castle or
sliding.

# A Chrysalis

chrysalis

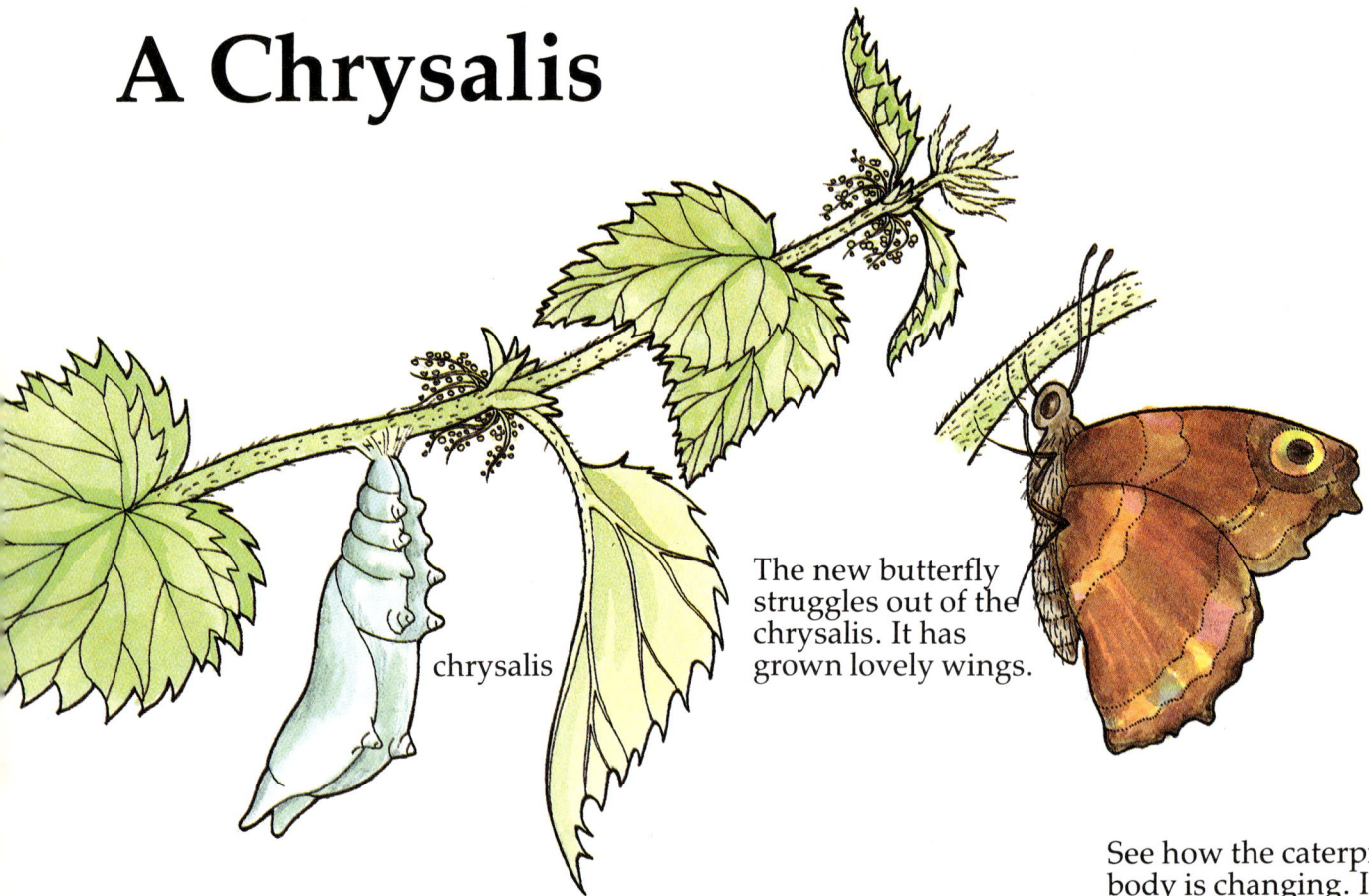

The new butterfly struggles out of the chrysalis. It has grown lovely wings.

This looks like a dead leaf on a branch.
But it is really a chrysalis.
A caterpillar made it.

See how the caterpillar's body is changing. It won't look like a caterpillar with lots of legs any more. It turns slowly into a butterfly with six legs.

Inside the chrysalis's cocoon, the caterpillar is changing into a beautiful butterfly.

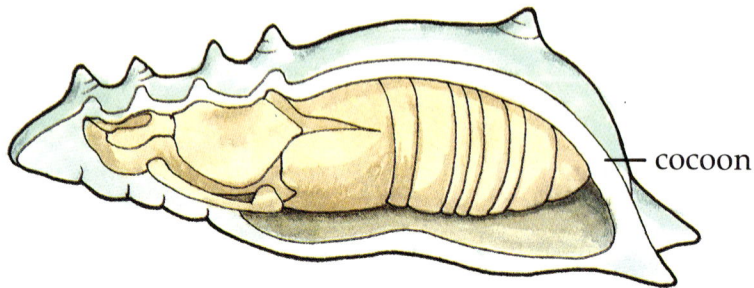

cocoon

**Make a paper butterfly**

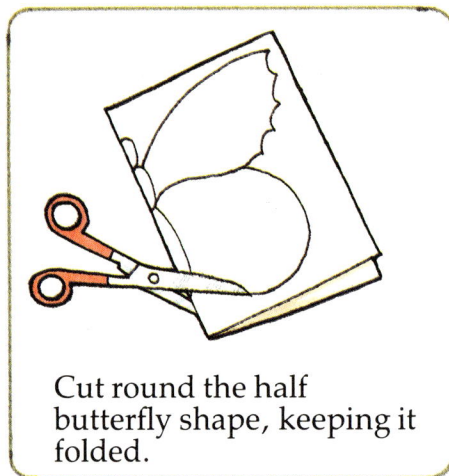

Fold a piece of paper in half. Draw half a butterfly shape on the folded edge.

Cut round the half butterfly shape, keeping it folded.

Flatten it out to make a whole butterfly. Paint a pattern on one half.

The beautiful butterfly flies up into the air.

Later the butterfly lays eggs.

The eggs hatch into grubs. Butterfly and moth grubs are called caterpillars.

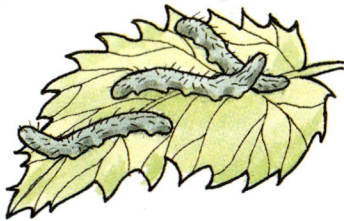

Later each caterpillar makes itself a cocoon, and turns into a chrysalis – and the whole story begins again!

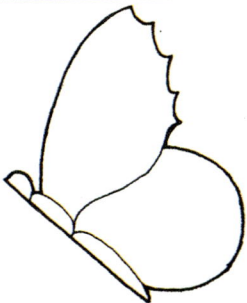

While the paint is still wet, fold the butterfly in half with the painted side inside.

Open it out, and see its lovely wings. The pattern is the same on both wings.

Make several butterflies. Stick them on to cotton and then on to a coat-hanger and hang it up.

# A Bird's Nest

Many birds build nests.
They lay their eggs in them.
Baby birds hatch from the eggs.
The mother and father birds
bring food to their babies.
Later the babies learn to fly.

This baby bird
has just hatched.
The nest is made
of grass and moss
woven together
with cobwebs.
It is lined with
feathers.

**What's inside an egg**

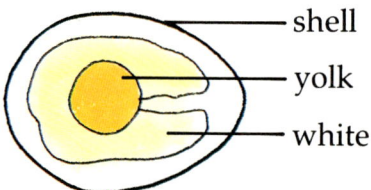

shell

yolk

white

As the baby bird grows inside the egg, it uses the yolk for food.

When it is big enough, the baby bird pecks its way out of the egg.

**What's inside a bird**
This is what the bones inside a bird look like.

If you find a bird's nest, do not go too close to it and do not let the birds see you watching them. You will frighten them. And never take birds' eggs. That is a cruel thing to do to a bird.

# Your Body

You cannot see what's inside your real body unless you have an X-ray. But . . .

red blood going from heart

blue blood going to heart

heart

lungs

kidneys

**breathing and blood systems**

**How your arm bends**

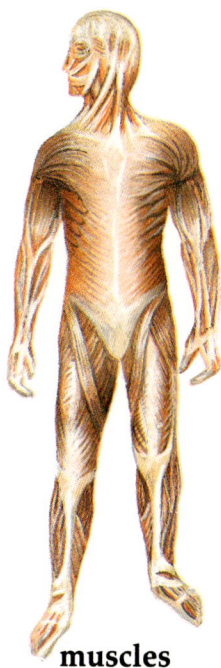

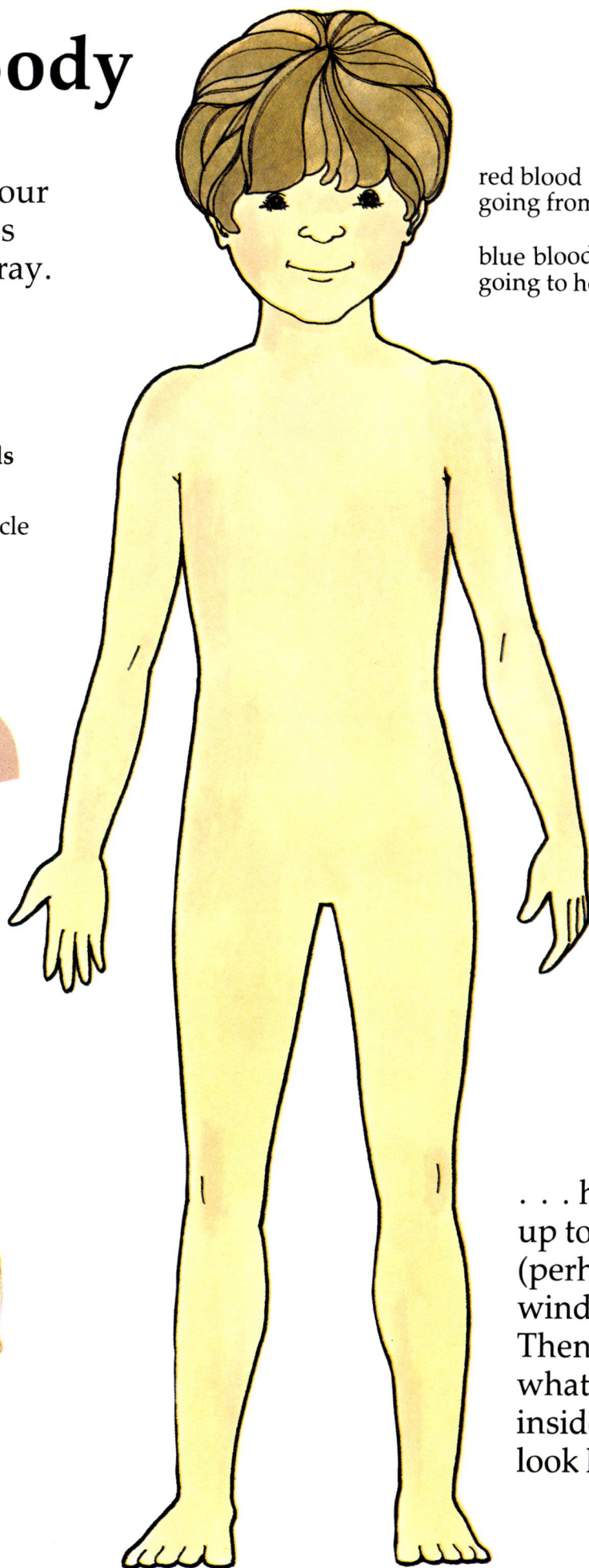

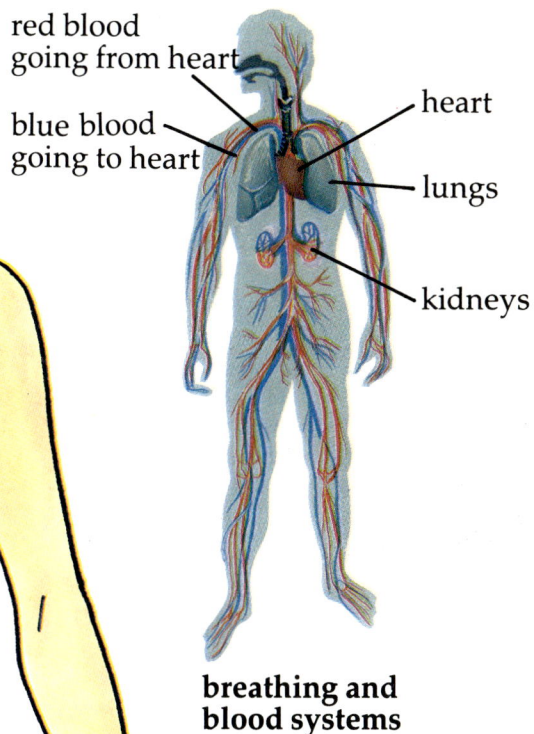

biceps muscle

triceps muscle

**muscles**

. . . hold this page up to the light (perhaps against a window pane). Then you'll see what the bones inside your body look like.

# Inside your body

All the bones inside your body are called your skeleton. Your skeleton holds you up. Without it, your soft body would collapse.

Each bone has a special name.

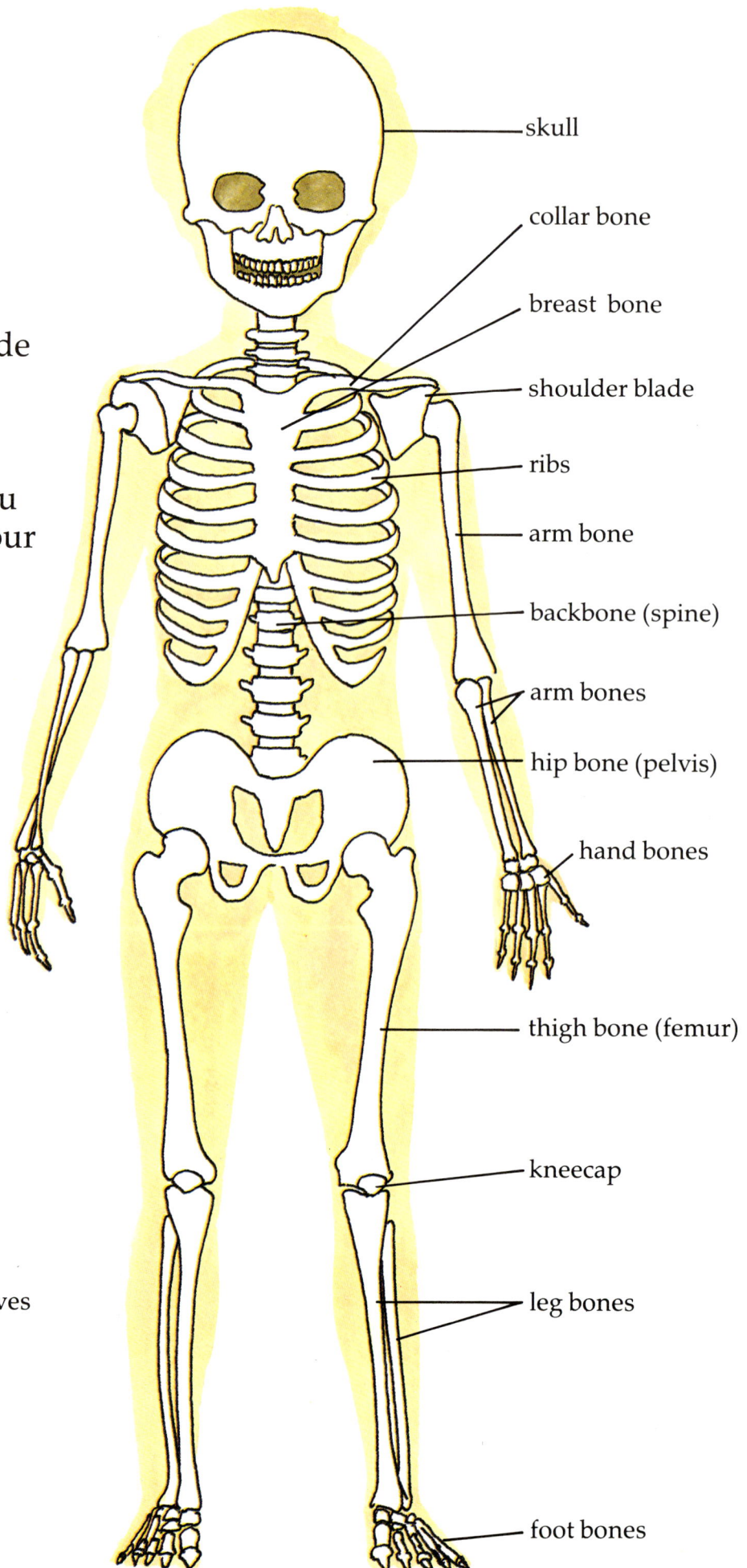

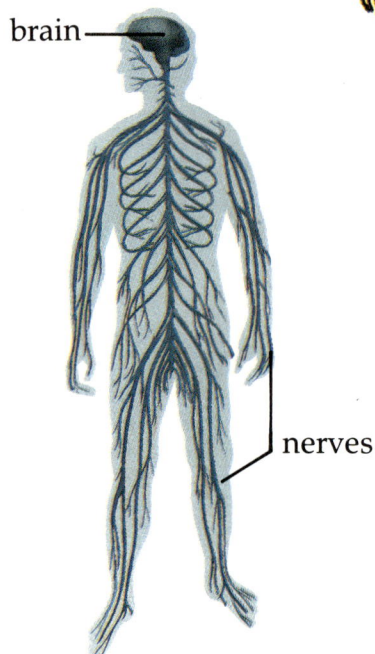

skull

collar bone

breast bone

shoulder blade

ribs

arm bone

backbone (spine)

arm bones

hip bone (pelvis)

hand bones

thigh bone (femur)

kneecap

leg bones

foot bones

brain

nerves

**brain and nerves**

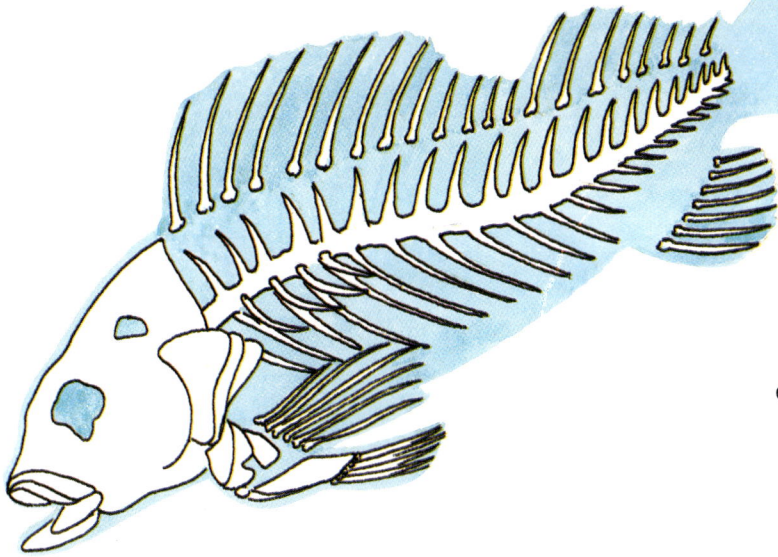
fish

**Teeth**

You can tell what animals eat by looking at their teeth. The cat has sharp teeth for eating meat.

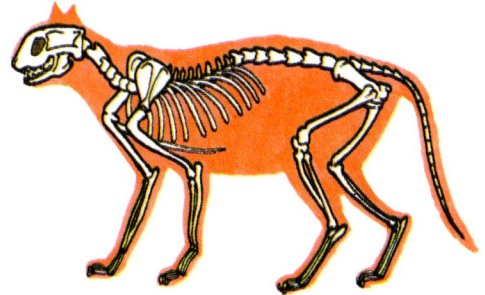
cat

dog

Look at the skeletons on this page. See how like each other they are. Can you see the spine, or backbone, in each one?

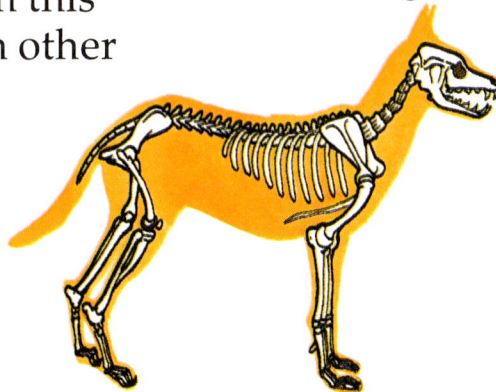

What kind of food does the dog eat? Look at its teeth.

rabbit

The rabbit has strong back teeth for chewing grass.

This dinosaur had little teeth for eating plants. He had to chew all day to fill his big body.

An oyster has a shell to protect its soft body. Some oysters grow pearls inside them.

Sometimes a bit of grit gets inside the oyster's body. The poor oyster doesn't like the feel of the grit so it grows a smooth pearly coat round it to stop it hurting.

dinosaur

# In Your Home

**Hall**

## Lock

To get inside your home you must turn a key in a lock.

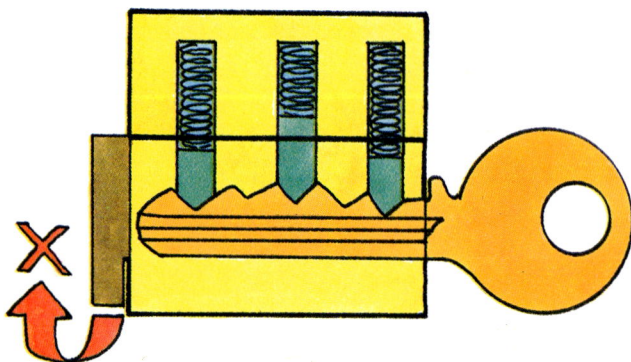

This key does not work.
This key does.

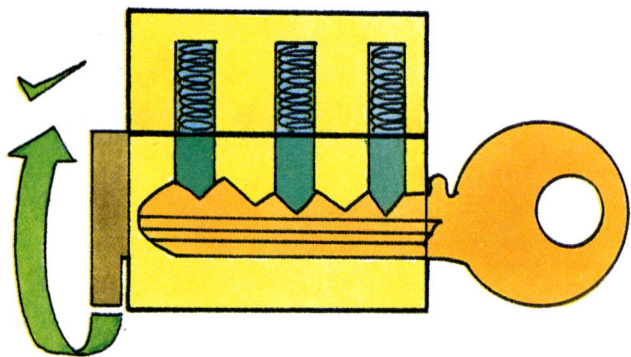

**Electric Light Bulb**

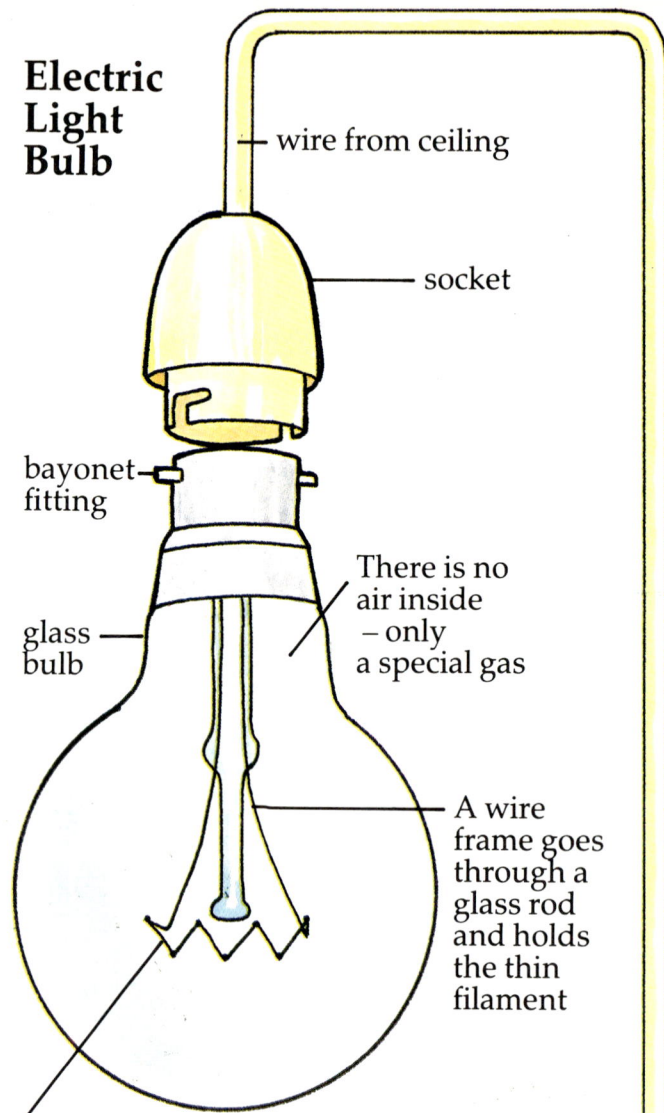

wire from ceiling

socket

bayonet fitting

There is no air inside – only a special gas

glass bulb

A wire frame goes through a glass rod and holds the thin filament

The electricity makes the filament so hot that it glows. But it does not melt because it is made of special metal.

The light works only when the wires make a complete circuit. When the switch is off there is a gap between the wires.

# Sitting Room

clock

television

telephone

piano

## Piano

Inside a piano there is a frame of metal wires called strings. The short strings make high notes. The long strings make low notes.

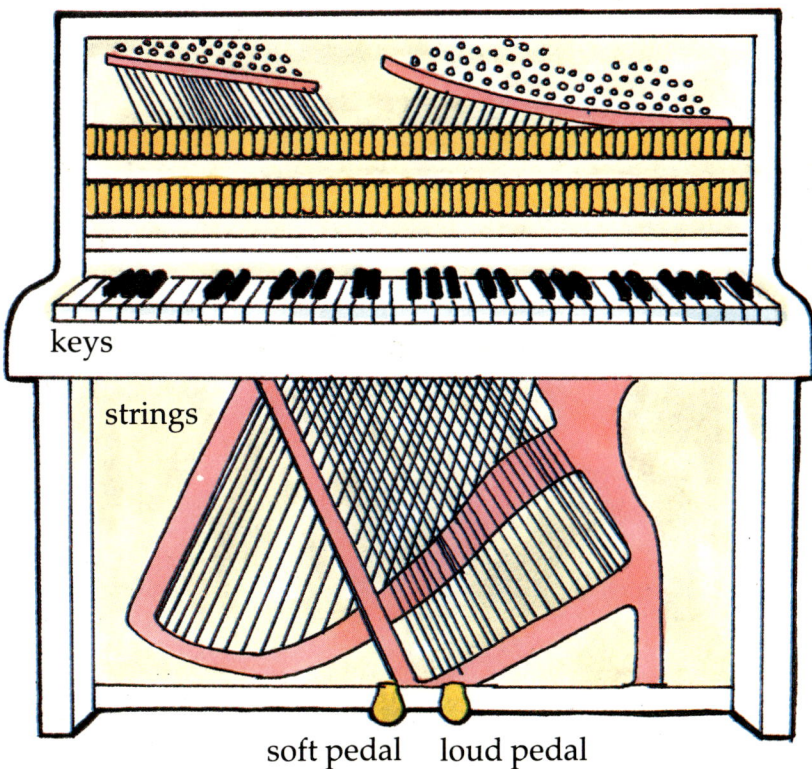

keys

strings

soft pedal    loud pedal

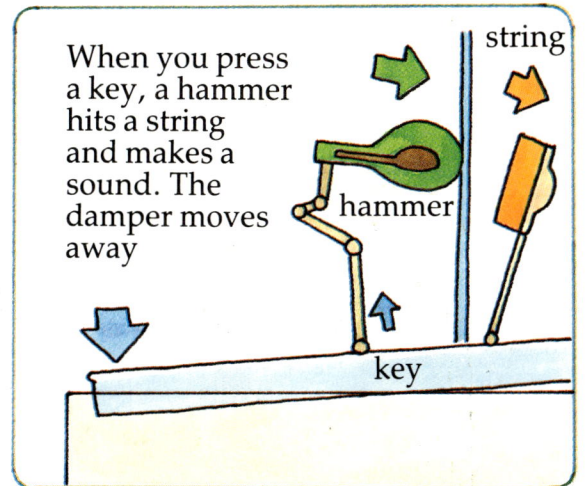

When you press a key, a hammer hits a string and makes a sound. The damper moves away

string

hammer

key

When you let the key go, the damper goes back and the sound stops.

damper

# Kitchen

vacuum flask

iron

washing machine

vacuum cleaner

liquidizer

squeezer

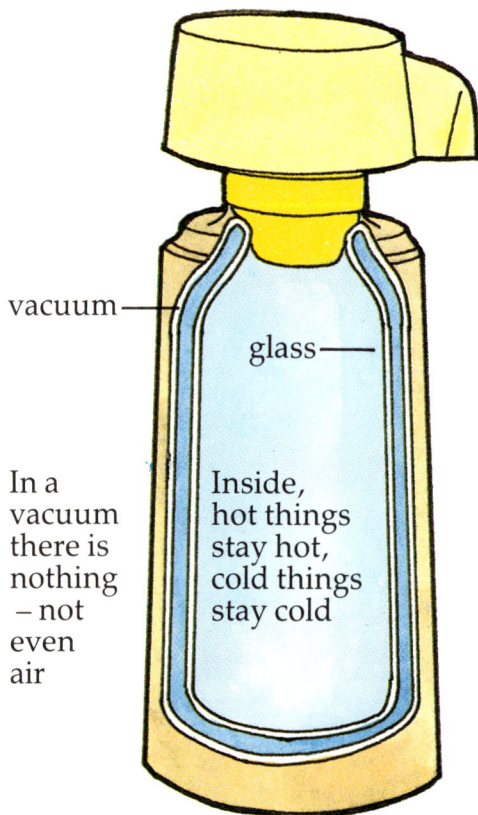

vacuum

glass

Inside, hot things stay hot, cold things stay cold

In a vacuum there is nothing – not even air

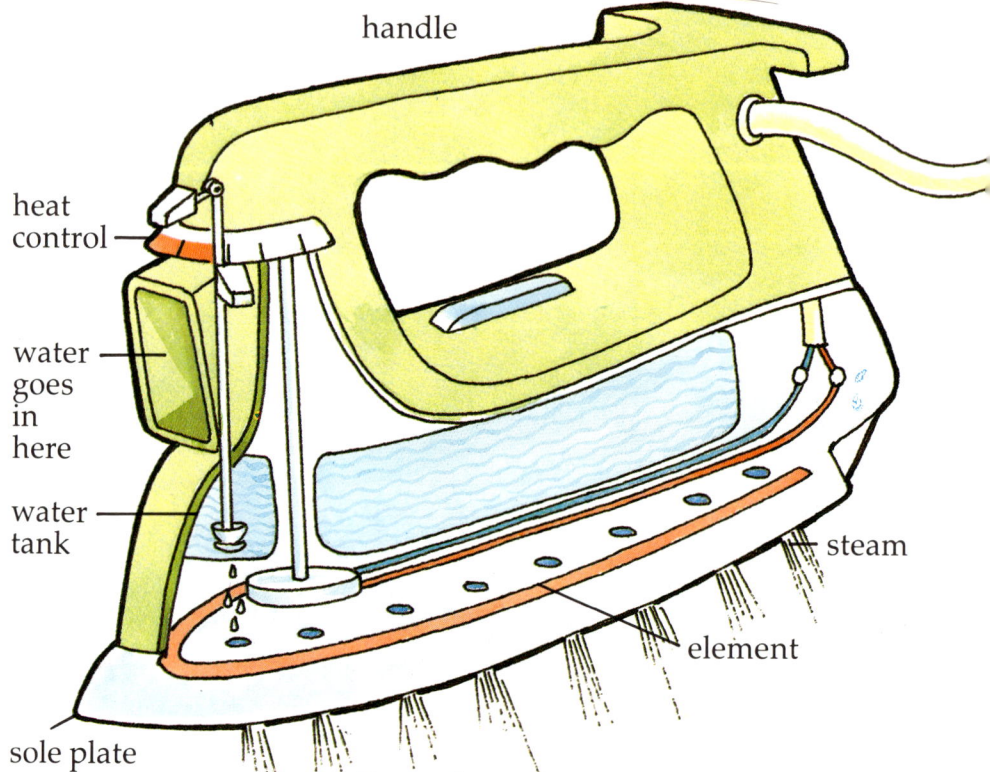

handle

heat control

water goes in here

water tank

sole plate

steam

element

## Vacuum flask

Heat needs something to conduct it from one place to another. Even air will do. In a vacuum there is nothing at all, so heat cannot get in or out of a vacuum flask.

## Steam iron

Hot irons press creases out of clothes. Some irons use steam to damp the creases. Electricity heats a metal plate called an element and turns the water to steam. A thermostat stops the iron getting too hot.

## Washing machine

The timer switches on the motor. The motor drives the pump which fills the machine with water. It also drives the agitator which washes and rinses the clothes by spinning the tub. The holes in the tub let out water during spinning.

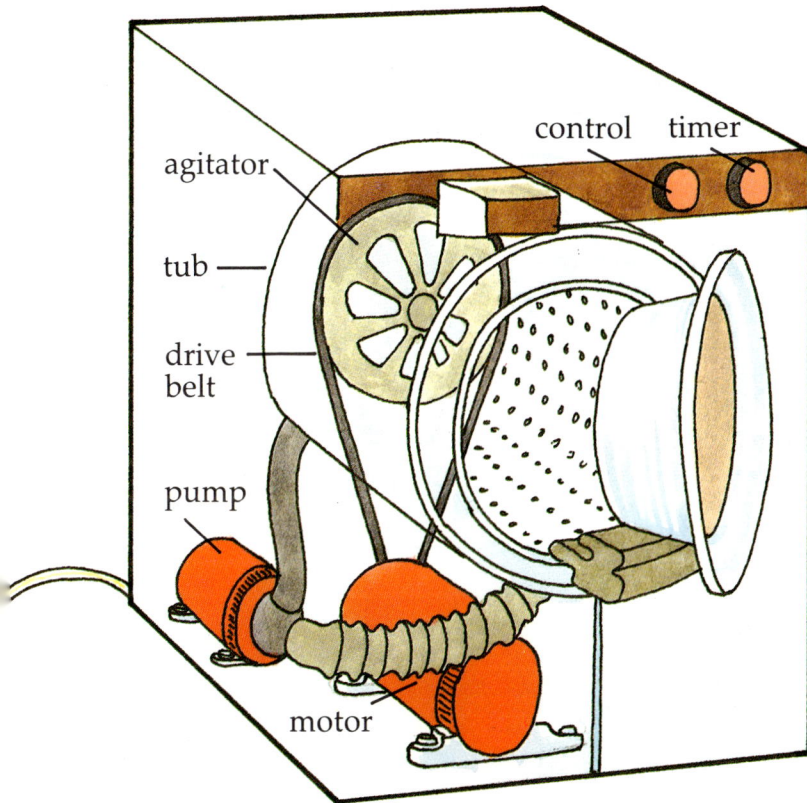

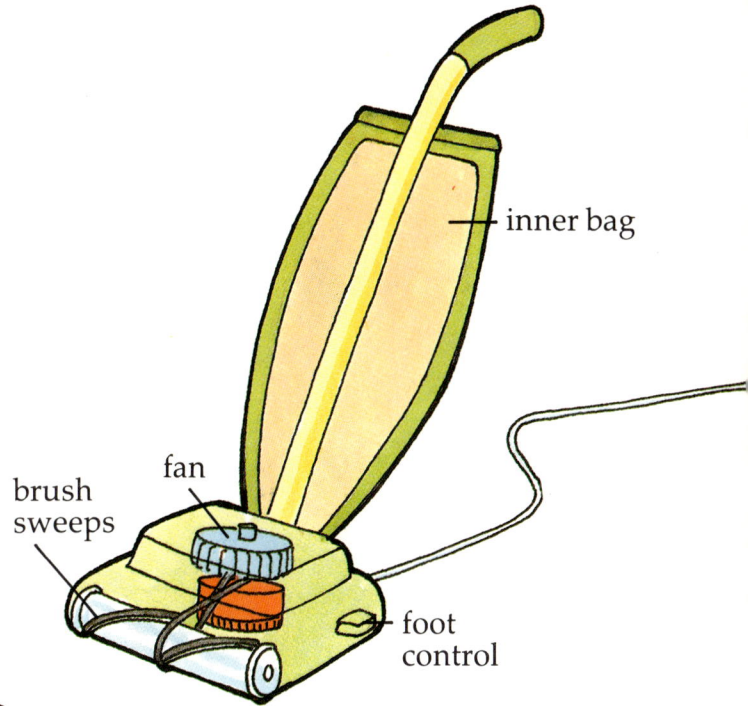

inner bag

brush sweeps

fan

foot control

agitator

control    timer

tub

drive belt

pump

motor

## Vacuum cleaner

The motor drives a fan which sucks in dust and dirt. The brush at the front loosens the dirt as it turns. The bag collects the dust.

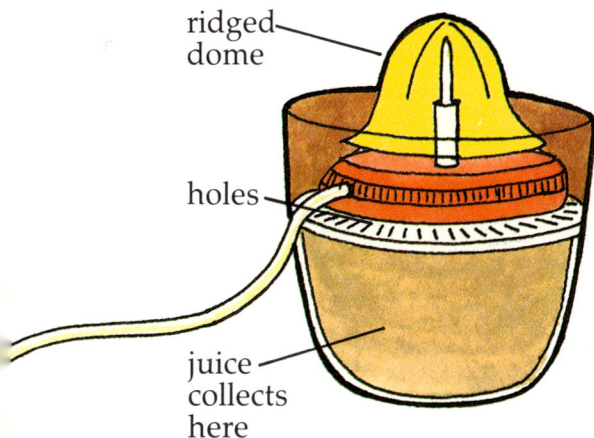

goblet

blades

motor

ridged dome

holes

juice collects here

## Juice squeezer

To get the juice from half an orange you press it over the ridged dome. The juice drops through little holes to the cup below.

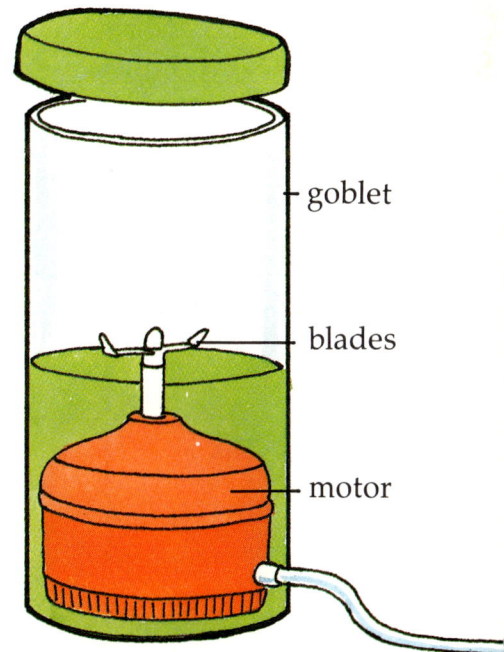

## Liquidizer

To blend solid and liquid food, metal blades whiz round and slice the food to pulp.

# Bedroom

hair-dryer

aerosol hair spray

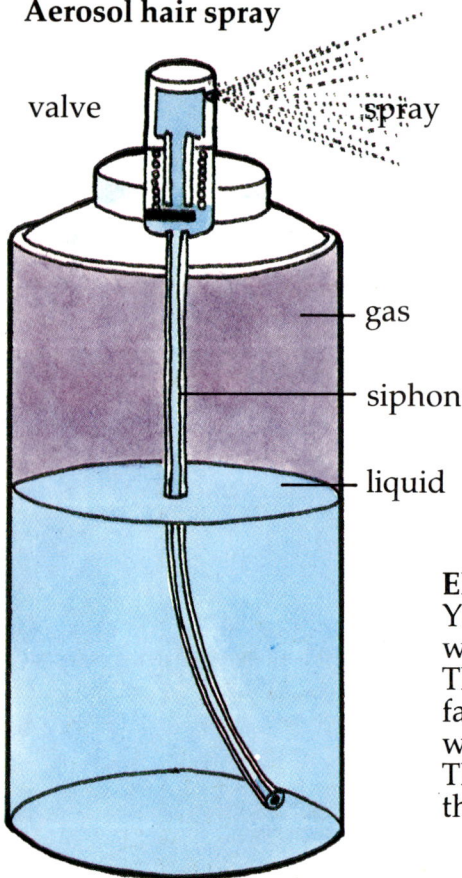

shaver

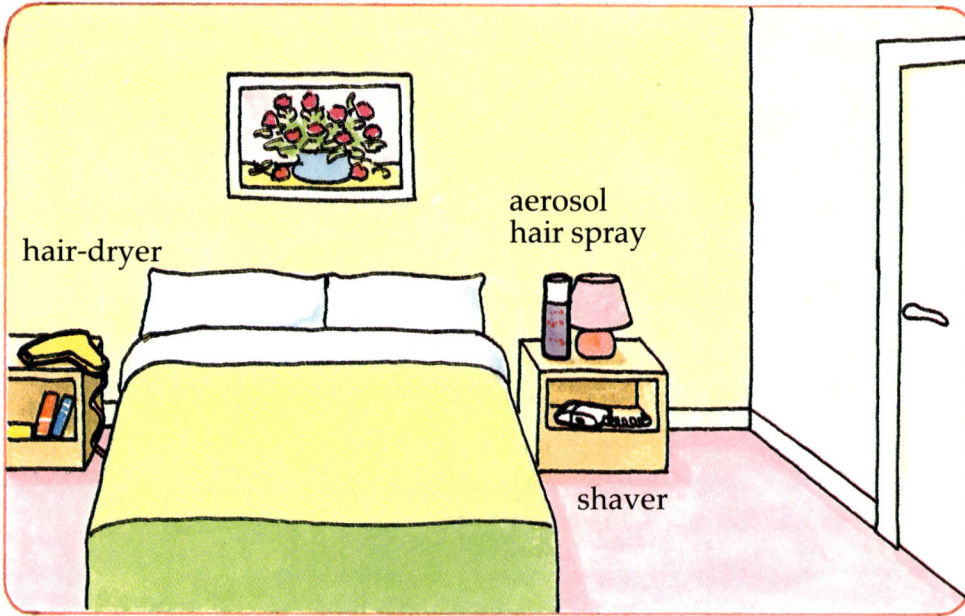

## Hair-dryer
A hair-dryer has a motor, a fan and a coiled element inside. Cold air is sucked in at the back and blown over the hot element. This heats the air, and hot air is blown out at the front.

fan

motor

coiled element

hot air out

wires

## Aerosol hair spray

valve

spray

gas

siphon

liquid

When you press the valve the hair spray is forced up the siphon and out of the tiny hole in the top.

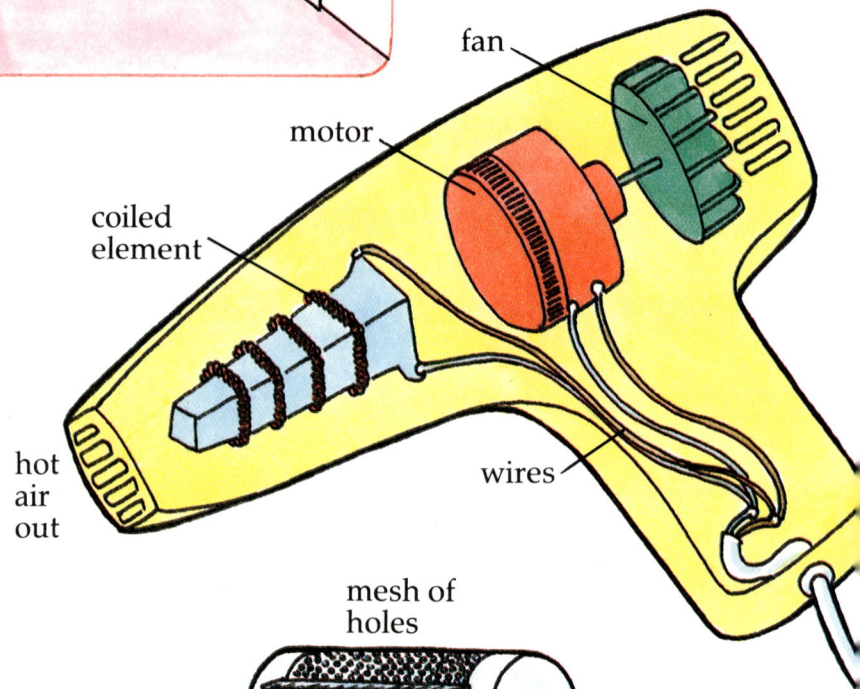

mesh of holes

blades

switch

motor

## Electric shaver
You cannot cut yourself with an electric shaver. The blades move very fast but they are covered with a mesh of holes. The hairs are cut off as they go into the holes.

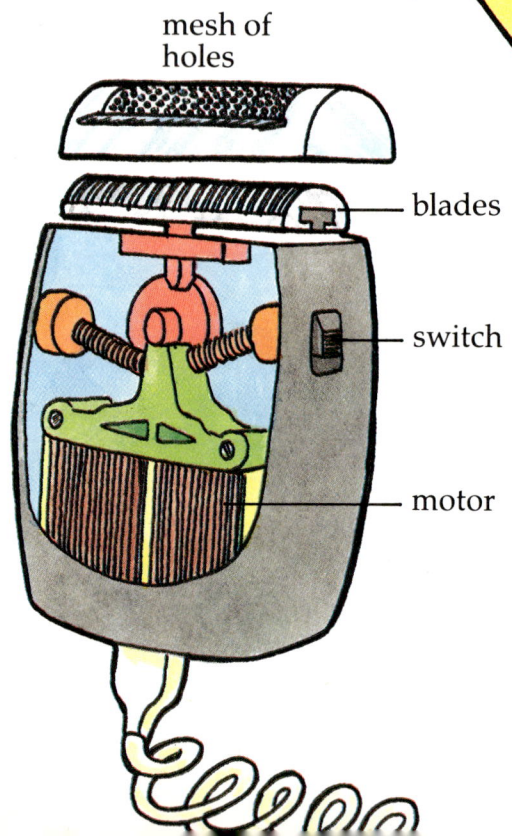

# Bathroom

cistern

tap

toothpaste

lavatory

## Tap
When you turn on a tap, you raise a spindle which opens a valve and lets water flow. When you turn off the tap the valve closes.

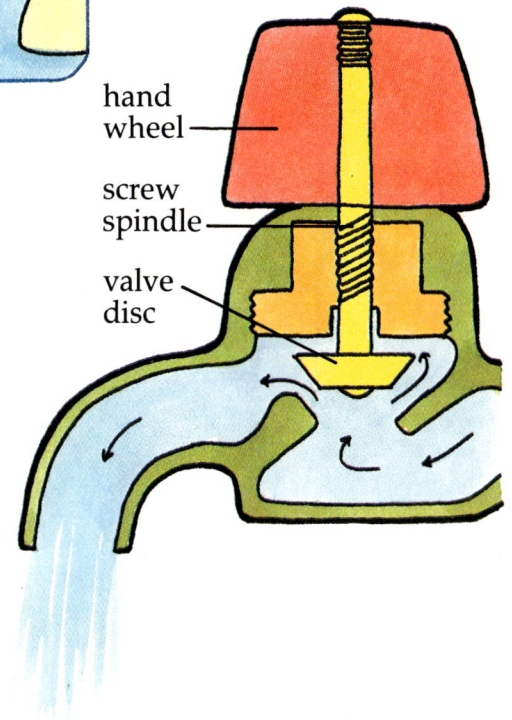

hand wheel

screw spindle

valve disc

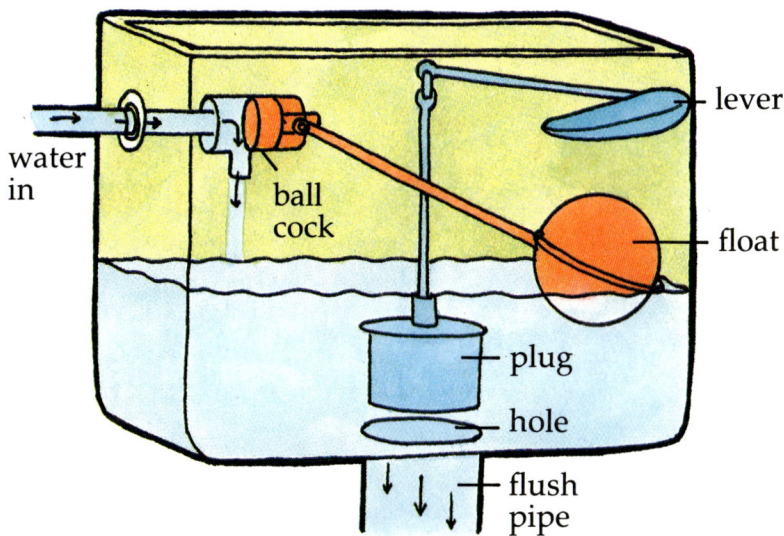

water in

ball cock

lever

float

plug

hole

flush pipe

## Cistern
When the lever is pressed the flush pipe is opened. The water flushes into the lavatory.
The float goes down and pulls open the opening to a water pipe so that the cistern fills up again.

## Toothpaste
Have you ever wondered how toothpaste can have stripes? You can see the secret in the picture.

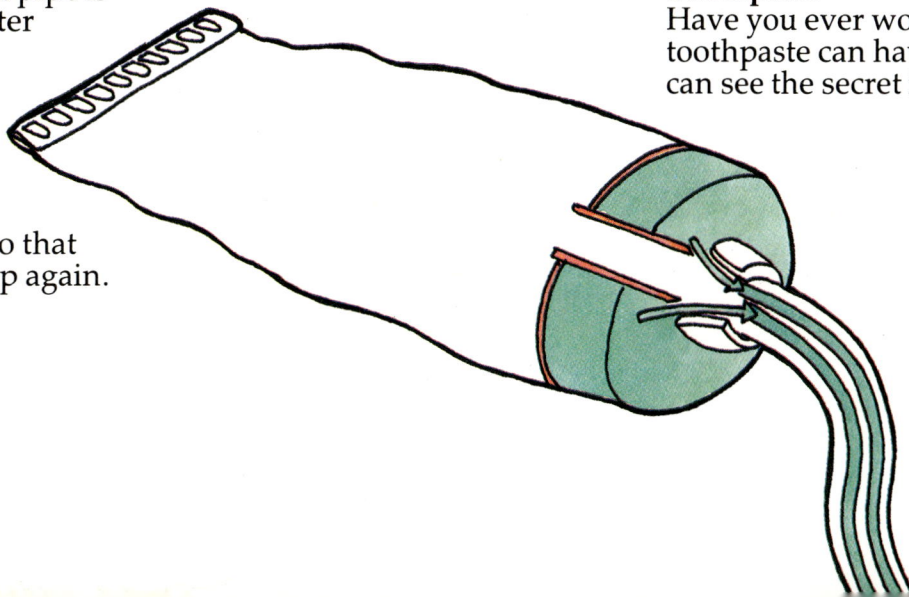

# A Clock

Clocks help us tell the time. They need power to make them go. They have to run at an exact rate.

**1** The key winds up the mainspring.

**2** The ratchet stops the spring unwinding all at once. It sticks in the notches on the ratchet wheel.

**3** As the mainspring slowly unwinds, it turns the big yellow wheel.

**4** The big yellow wheel turns the little red wheel.

**5** The little red wheel turns the shaft. The shaft turns the minute hand and the little mauve wheel.

## Wind-up clock

This wind-up clock has springs and wheels to make it go.

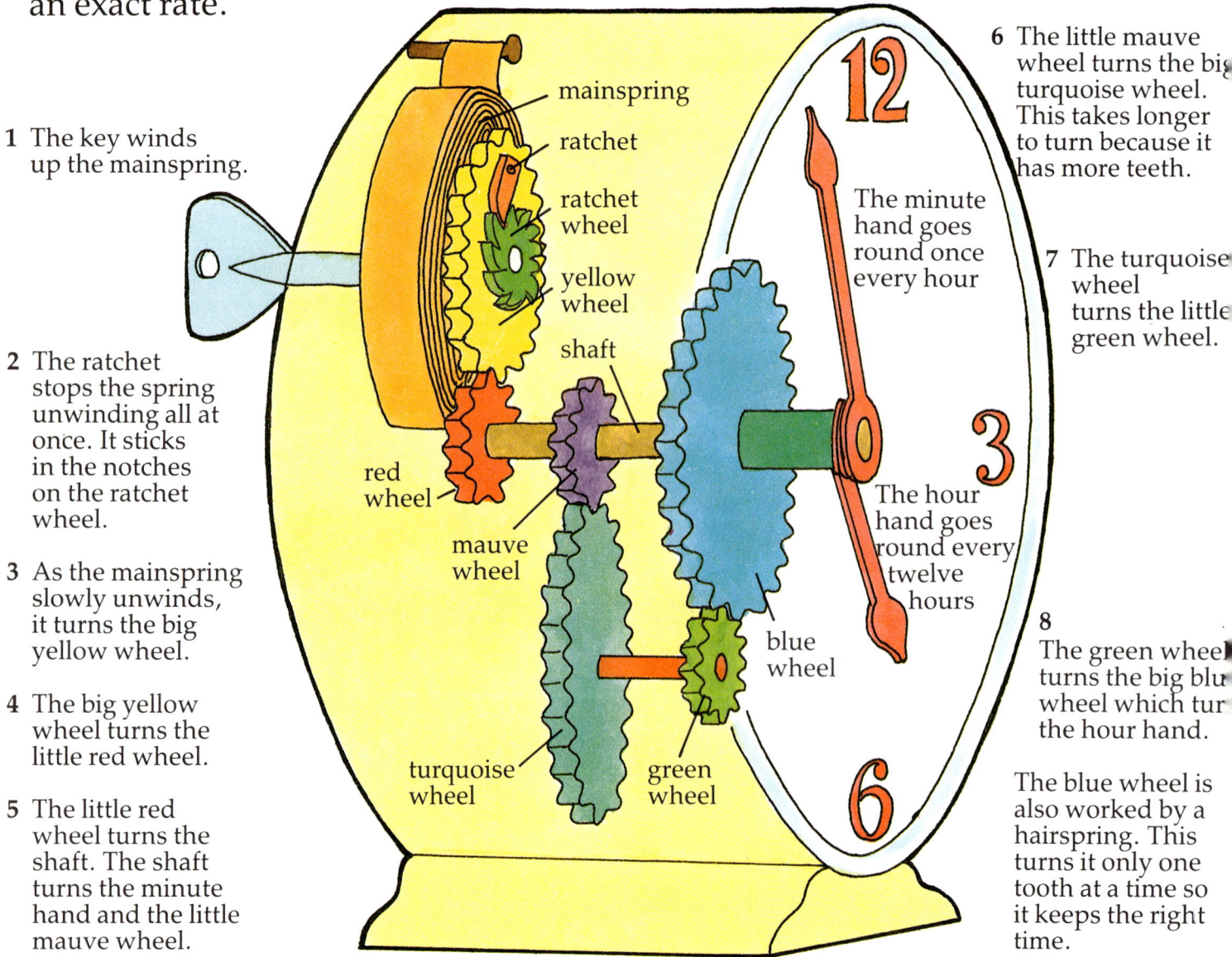

mainspring

ratchet

ratchet wheel

yellow wheel

shaft

red wheel

mauve wheel

turquoise wheel

green wheel

blue wheel

The minute hand goes round once every hour

The hour hand goes round every twelve hours

**6** The little mauve wheel turns the big turquoise wheel. This takes longer to turn because it has more teeth.

**7** The turquoise wheel turns the little green wheel.

**8** The green wheel turns the big blue wheel which turns the hour hand.

The blue wheel is also worked by a hairspring. This turns it only one tooth at a time so it keeps the right time.

---

**Do you know how to tell the time?**

Five o'clock

Ten minutes past five

The little hand shows what hour it is. The big hand shows how many minutes past the hour it is. Some clocks have a third hand that tells the seconds too. There are 60 seconds in a minute, 60 minutes in an hour, and 24 hours in a day and night.

## Cuckoo clock

This is a pendulum clock. The pendulum swings back and forth. The heavy weights cause wheels inside to move like those in a wind-up clock. The pendulum controls the speed at which they turn.

The cuckoo is on a spring that shoots out on the hour.

pendulum

## Digital watch

This digital watch is worked by a quartz crystal. It shows the time in numbers (digits).

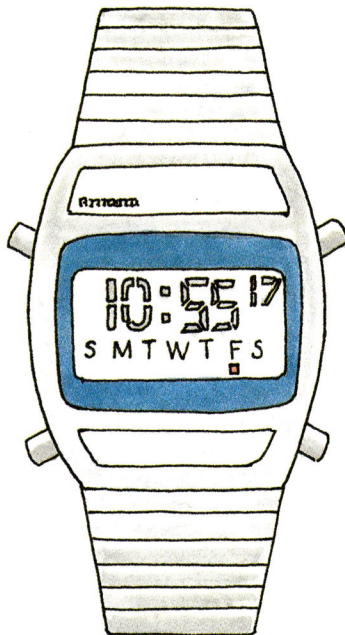

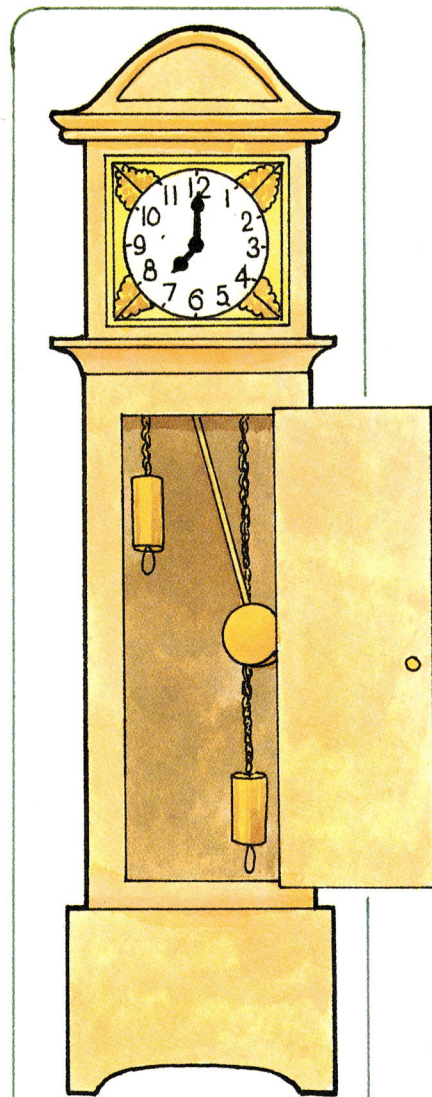

## Grandfather clock

This is worked by weights and a pendulum. To start it you pull one weight as far as it will go and make the pendulum swing.

**What time do these clocks say?**

## Electric clock

This is the back of an electric clock. It works with a battery.

# A Telephone

When you talk on the telephone to someone a long way away, the telephone changes the sounds of your voice into electrical signals.

When you dial a number you send a set of electrical signals along the wire to the exchange.

When someone dials your number electrical signals make the bell ring in your telephone.

metal plate

earpiece (receiver)

magnet

2 The other person's telephone changes the electrical signals back into sounds he can hear. The earpiece of the phone has a piece of metal. Behind it is a magnet. The changing electric current makes the magnet move the metal to and fro, so the other person can hear what you are saying.

mouthpiece (transmitter)

metal plate

carbon granules

Sounds go along a wire to a.

number

dial

bell

1 Inside the mouthpiece there is a piece of metal and some powder called carbon granules. The sound of your voice going up and down makes the metal vibrate and press against the carbon granules. Electricity passes through the granules. The amount of electricity going through changes with each sound you make.

dead matchstick

yoghurt pot

long piece of string

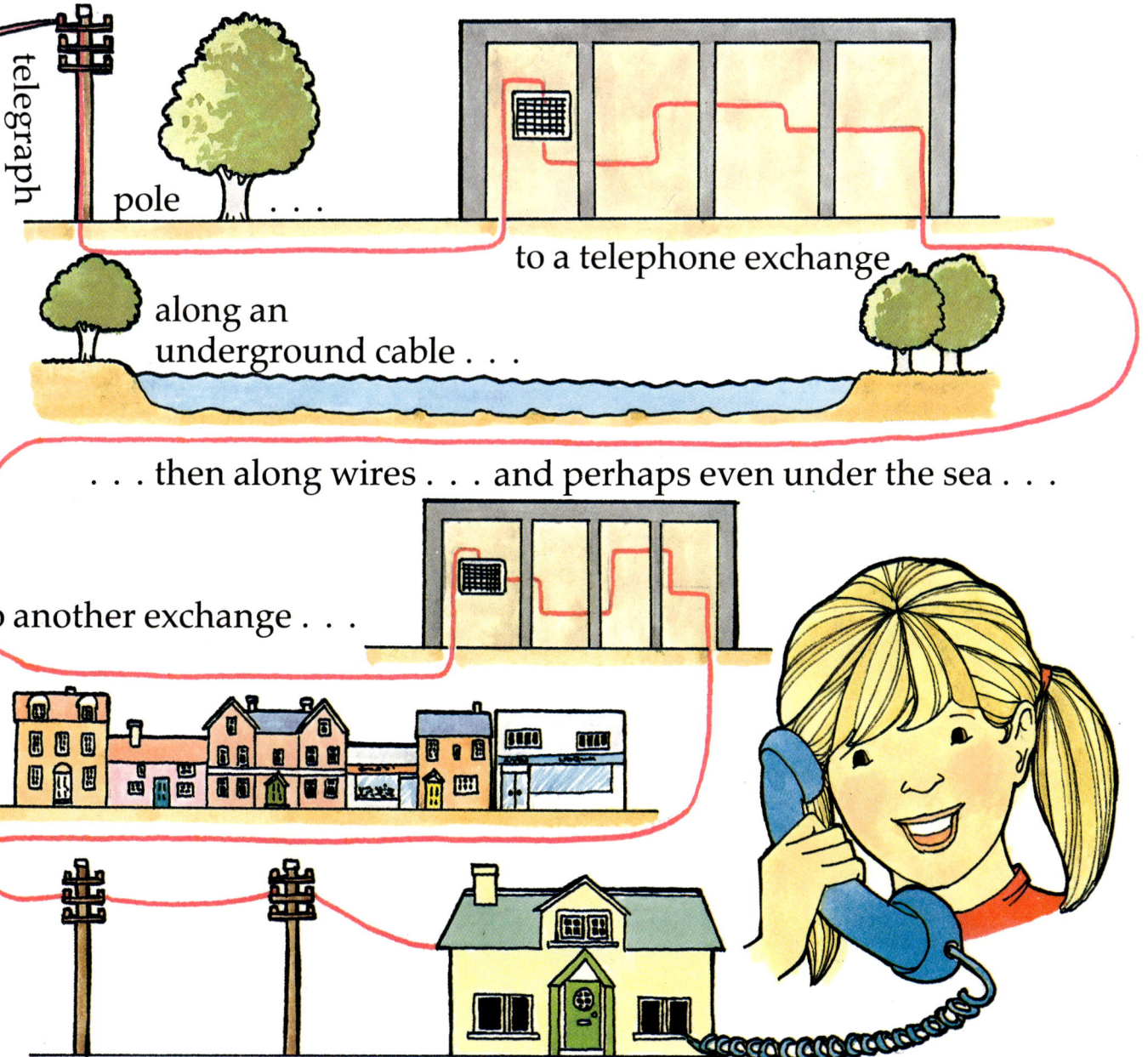

**Make a string telephone**
Thread a long piece of string through the
bottoms of two yoghurt pots. Tie each end to a
dead matchstick and pull the string very tight.
Talk into one pot and see if your friend can
hear you in the other pot. See how long you
can make the string and still hear each other.

telegraph

pole . . .

to a telephone exchange

along an
underground cable . . .

. . . then along wires . . . and perhaps even under the sea . . .

to another exchange . . .

. . . then up the pole . . . and along to your house.

# A Television Studio

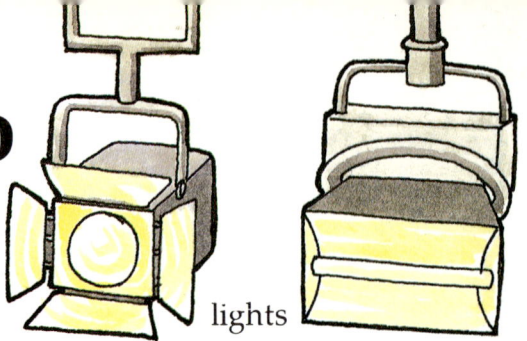

lights

Studios have many lights and wires.

A TV programme usually starts in a studio.

boom microphone

cable

Cameramen take moving pictures of the actors. They can hear the director through headsets.

Sound engineers record the music and the actors' voices on microphones.

head set

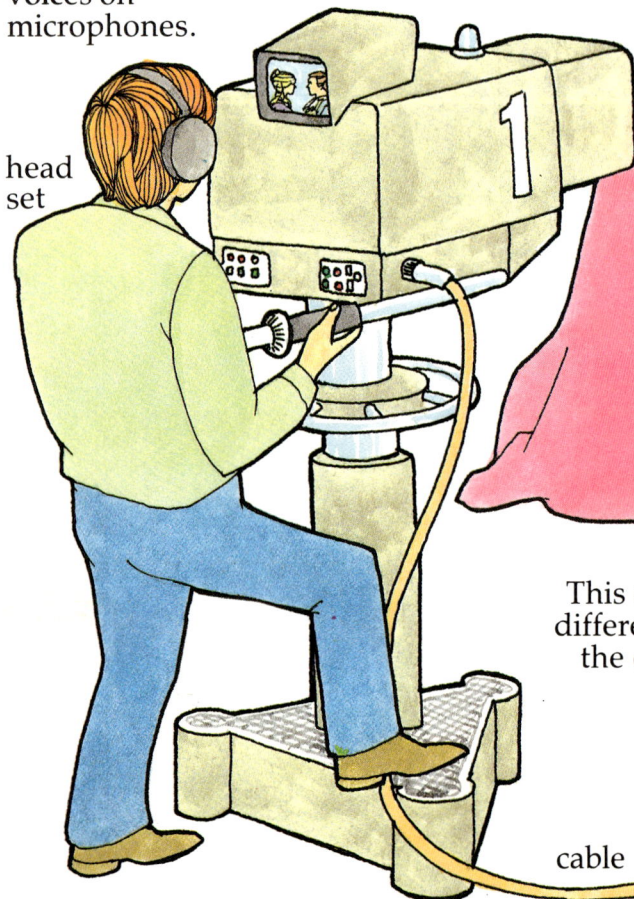

This camera sees a different view from the other camera.

The floor manager keeps everything in the studio going smoothly.

cable

**Control booth**

In the control booth, the monitor sets show what each camera is filming. The director decides which view you see on your TV screen. The vision mixer works the knobs on the control desk.

1　2　3　4

5　6　7　8

sound booth

vision mixer

director

control desk

The picture is sent from the control booth by cable to the transmitter on a high hill. Then the transmitter sends the picture to your TV aerial.

The picture (called the signal) goes through the air – you cannot see it yet. The TV aerial picks up the signal and passes it to the TV set. The tube in the set changes the signal to a picture you can see on your screen. Colours are made by mixing red, green and blue light.

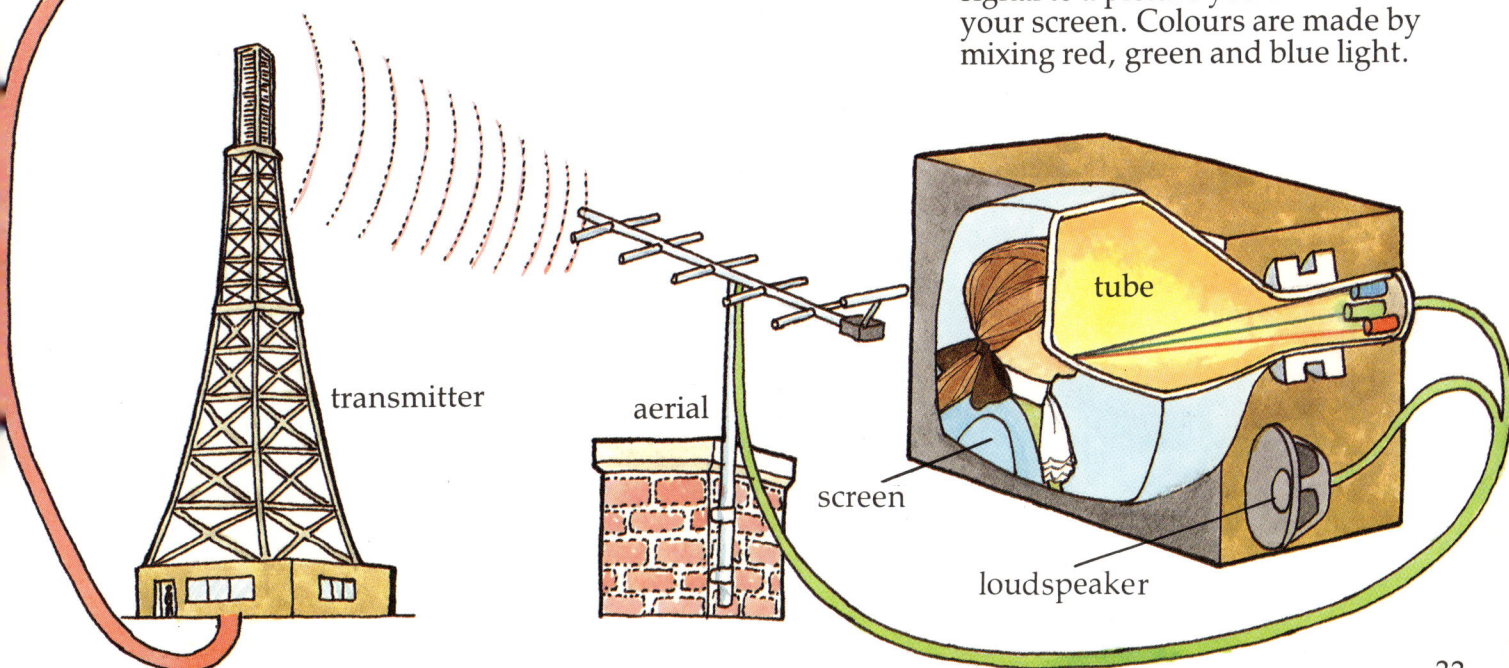

transmitter

aerial

tube

screen

loudspeaker

# A Supermarket

Supermarkets are very big food shops.

People take the goods off the shelves themselves.

They pay for their goods at the check-out.

Delivery lorries bring goods to the loading bay.

delivery lorries

They are taken to the stock room on forklift trucks.

forklift truck

Prices are marked on goods by a gun

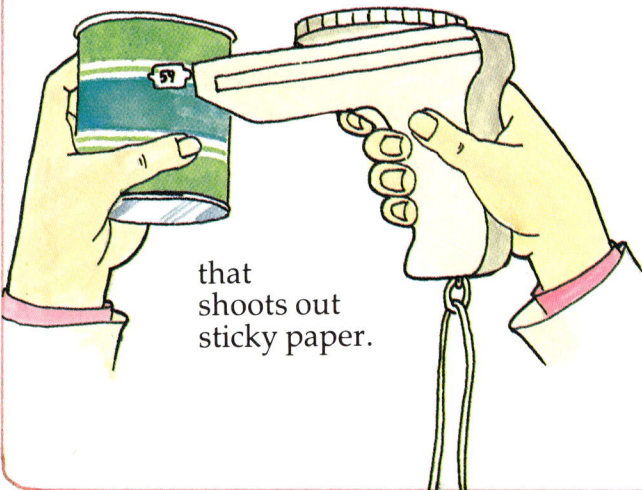

that shoots out sticky paper.

Goods are stacked on the shelves.

# Look for all these things when you go shopping.

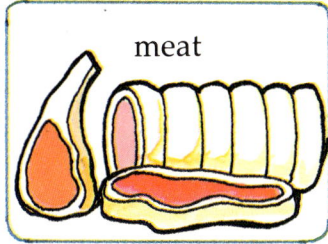

| meat | fish | poultry | bread and cakes |
|---|---|---|---|

| tinned food | delicatessen | fruit | vegetables |
|---|---|---|---|

| wine and beer | soft drinks | tea and coffee | soaps |
|---|---|---|---|

| frozen food | cleaning stuff | sweets | clothes |
|---|---|---|---|

The electric till at the check-out adds up all the prices and prints them on a long roll of paper.

check-out

basket          trolley

# A Building Site

On building sites, workers and machines move earth, dig big holes for foundations and put up buildings.

**Crane**
The big crane picks up a heavy object, hoists it high above the site, swings round and puts it down where it is needed.

jib

girder

cab

hook

counterweights

The cement mixer churns sand, cement, stones and water to make concrete.

A hard hat protects the worker's head if something heavy falls down.

foundations

carpenter

tower

pneumatic drill

view hole

pile of bricks

hoarding

wheelbarrow

bricklayer

scaffolding

Mortar is a mixture of sand, cement and water.

hod

A JCB crawler-excavator can move backwards and forwards. The bucket at the front can dig and the scoop at the back can move and carry lots of rubble.

This is a JCB crawler-excavator

cab

boom

The front bucket scoops up earth.

wheels

Legs keep the machine steady on rough ground.

# A Chocolate Factory

Chocolate comes from cocoa beans.
Cocoa trees grow in hot countries.
Big pods grow on the tree trunks.
The cocoa beans are inside the pods.

When the pods are ripe, workers
cut them open. They dry the beans
in a big pile.

Workers put the beans into sacks.
A big ship takes them to countries
which make chocolate.

A lorry takes the sacks of beans to
the chocolate factory.

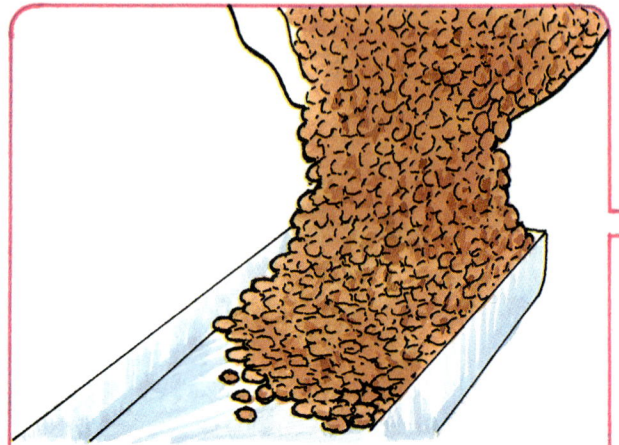

Inside the factory, the beans go down
a chute.

Rollers grind the mixture smooth.

Some chocolate is made into bars.

chocolate bar

A machine cleans them.

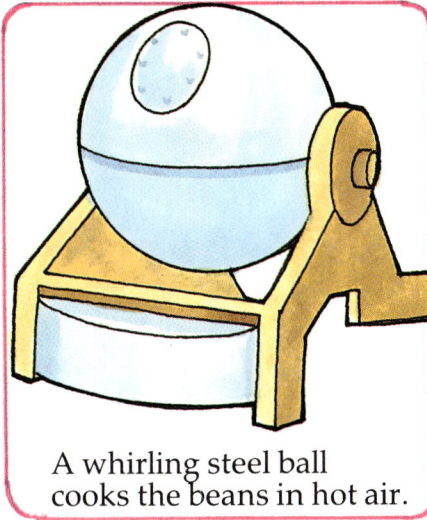

A whirling steel ball cooks the beans in hot air.

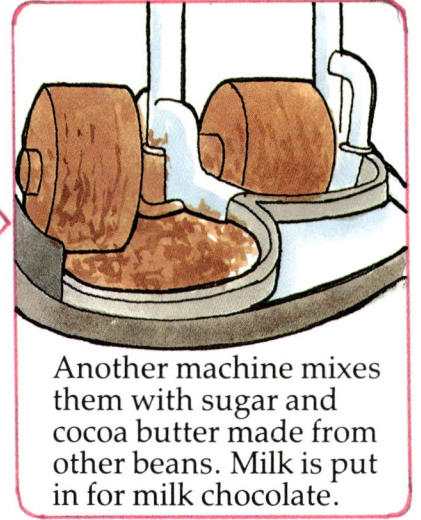

Another machine mixes them with sugar and cocoa butter made from other beans. Milk is put in for milk chocolate.

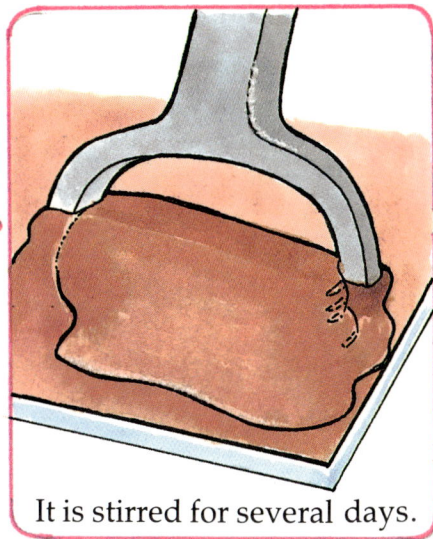

It is stirred for several days.

A special machine makes the mixture nice and shiny.

Some chocolate is made into little chocolates. Runny chocolate is poured over fruit or nut centres.

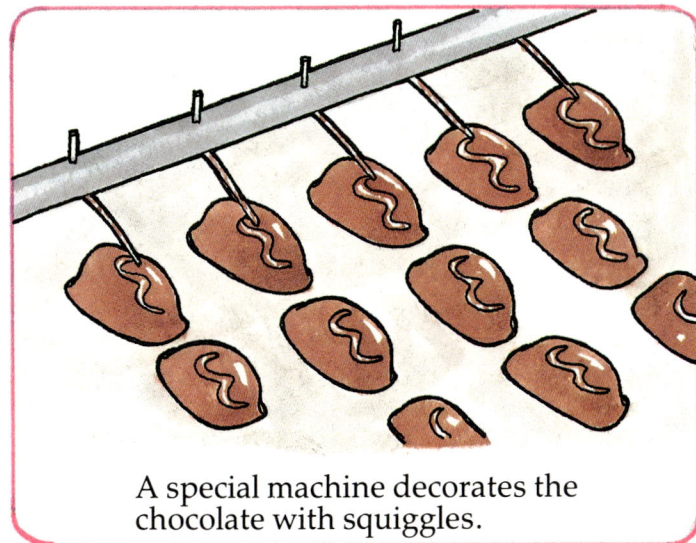

A special machine decorates the chocolate with squiggles.

Smarties are little chocolate buttons. They are made between big rollers and covered with sugar and colours.

box of chocolates

smarties

# An Airport

Many people work at an airport.

Aircraft are parked in hangars.

fuel tanks

Planes take off from the main runway.

plane waiting to take off

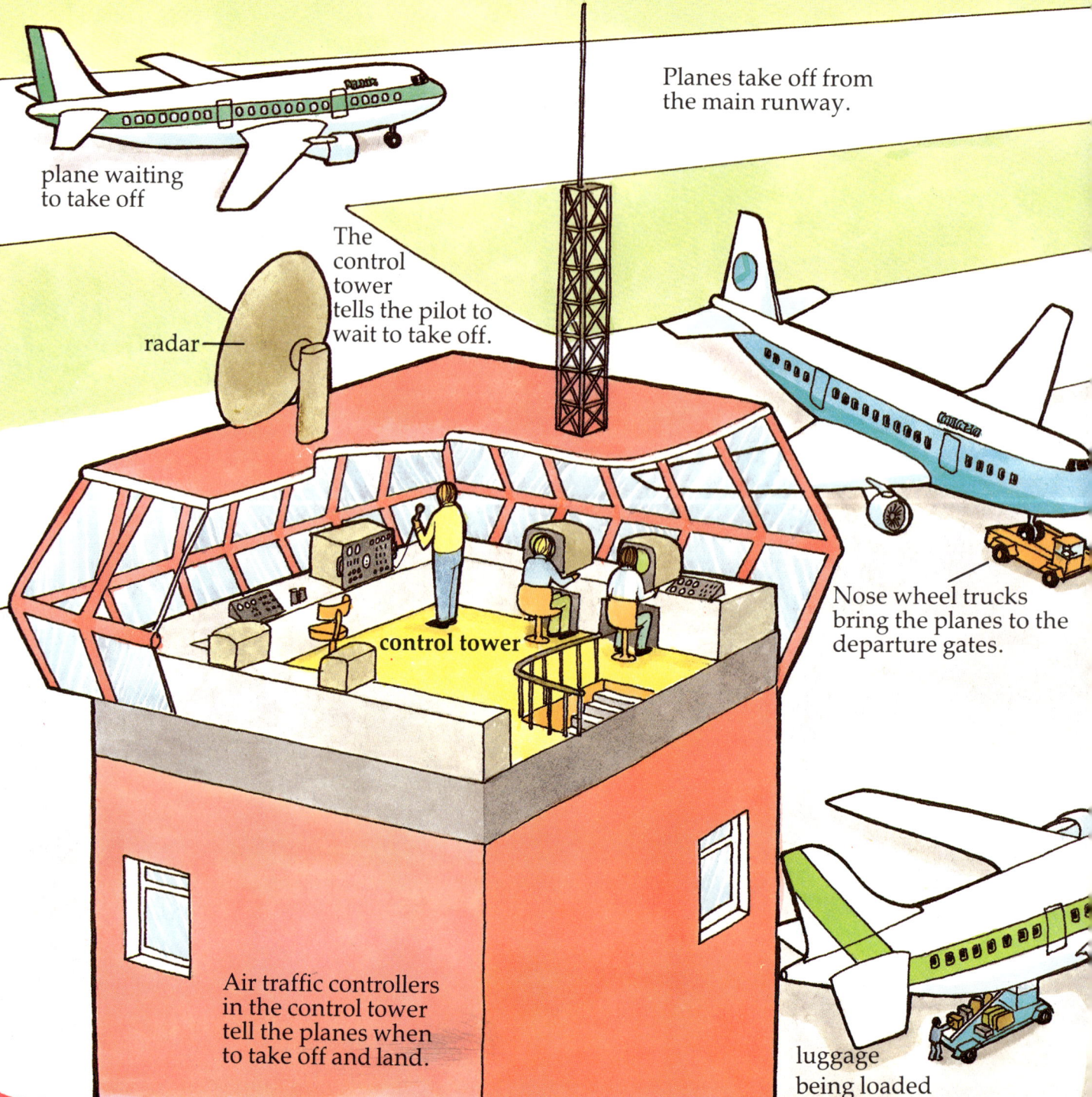

The control tower tells the pilot to wait to take off.

radar

control tower

Nose wheel trucks bring the planes to the departure gates.

Air traffic controllers in the control tower tell the planes when to take off and land.

luggage being loaded

An airport is a very busy place.
Aeroplanes take off and land
there all the time.

Parts are repaired in
the workshop.

plane taking off

windsock

main runway

observation deck

ticket sales

flight
information

passenger terminal

offices

taxiway

restaurants

bank

car hire

apron

shop

departure
lounge

security
checks

check-in
desks

parking bay

telephones

way in

jetty

passport
control

car park

fuel truck

food truck

Everyone comes and
goes from the
passenger terminal.

# A Castle

Long ago rich lords lived in castles. A castle was built on a small hill called a motte. High walls were built all around it. When enemies attacked, all the people in the village drove their animals inside the castle walls. They were safer there. But often the enemy stopped them coming out again. They laid siege to the castle to starve the people into surrender.

**Make a castle**
Stick four cardboard tubes on to a small box with sticky tape. Kitchen foil tubes are good with a big tissue or shoe box. Paint on doors and windows and make a flag for the top.

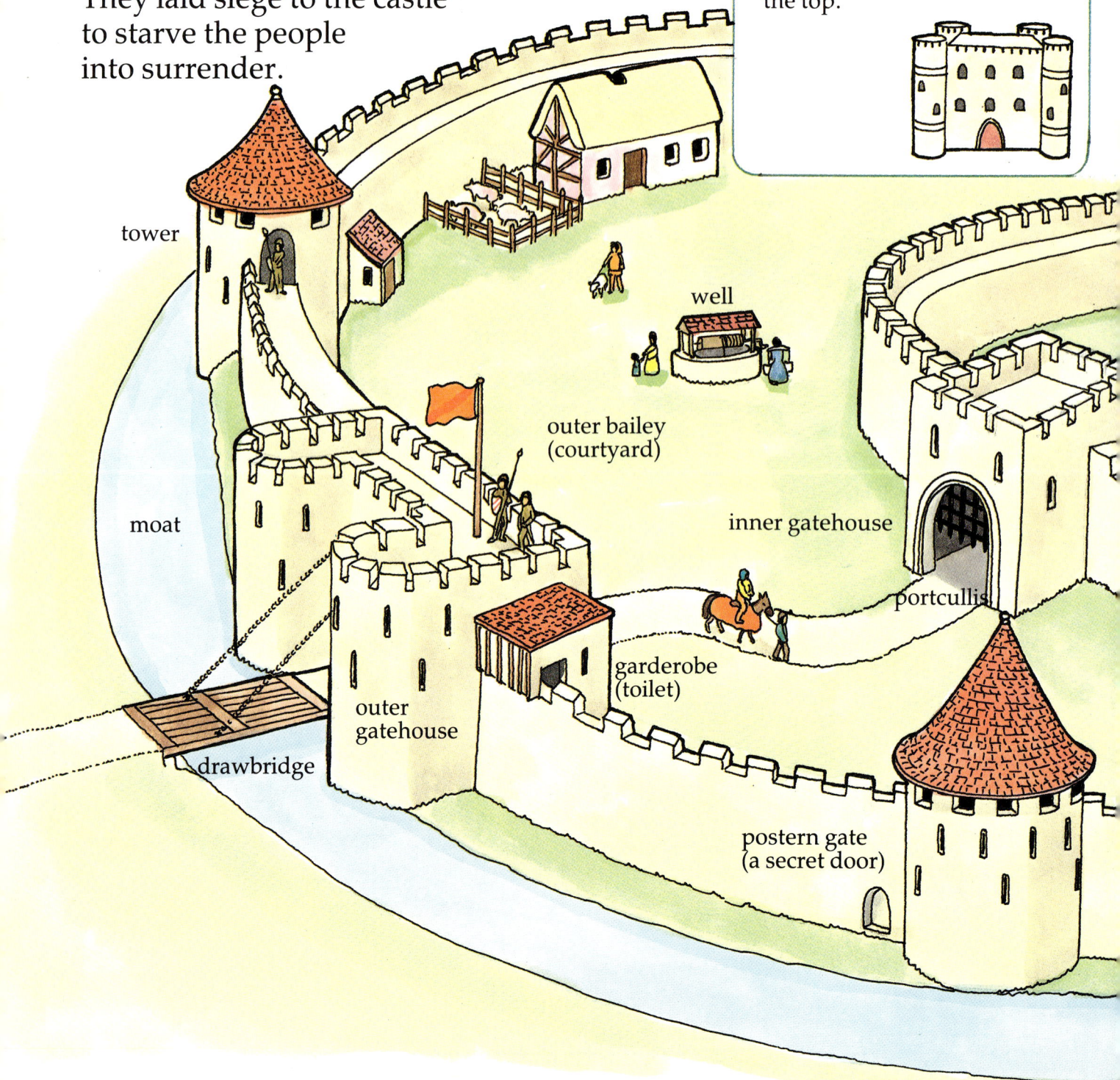

tower

well

moat

outer bailey (courtyard)

inner gatehouse

portcullis

garderobe (toilet)

outer gatehouse

drawbridge

postern gate (a secret door)

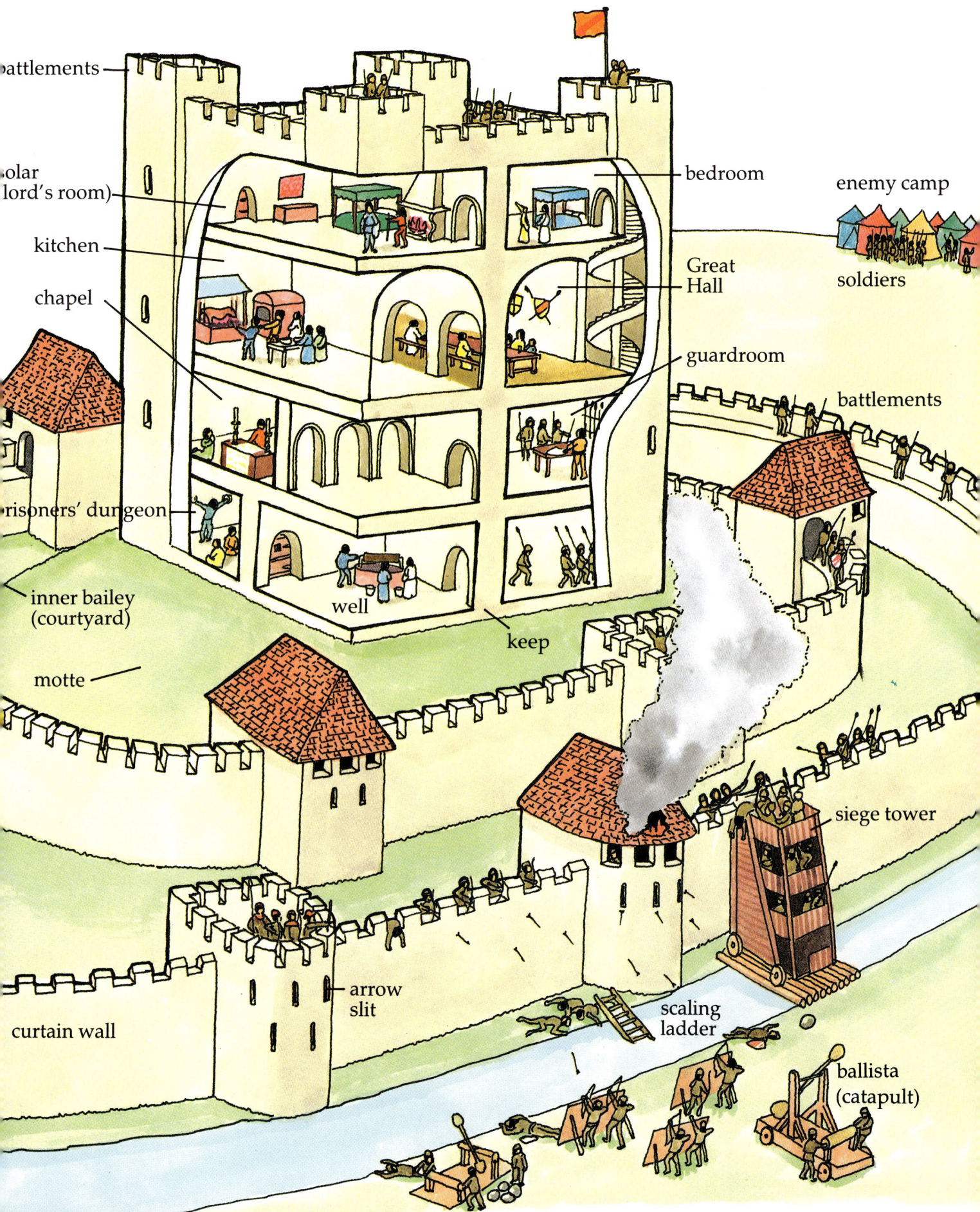

battlements

solar
(lord's room)

kitchen

chapel

prisoners' dungeon

inner bailey
(courtyard)

motte

well

keep

curtain wall

arrow
slit

bedroom

enemy camp

soldiers

Great
Hall

guardroom

battlements

siege tower

scaling
ladder

ballista
(catapult)

# An Escalator

Escalators are moving staircases. People step on to them to go up and down between floors.
The steps are pulled up or down by a chain.
A motor drives the chain.

This is an UP escalator. A DOWN escalator works in the same way, but the steps go down instead of up.

**Do you know**
- The longest escalators in the world are in Russia. On the Leningrad Underground they go up over 59 metres.
- The fastest ordinary passenger lifts in the world are in Japan. They move at around 609 metres a minute (36 kilometres an hour).
- Ears start popping in lifts around 16 kilometres an hour!

Always hold the handrail.

The steps come out of a slot in the floor. They are flat so people can get on to them easily.

The steps fold flat to go down to the bottom again.

The chain goes round and round and round.

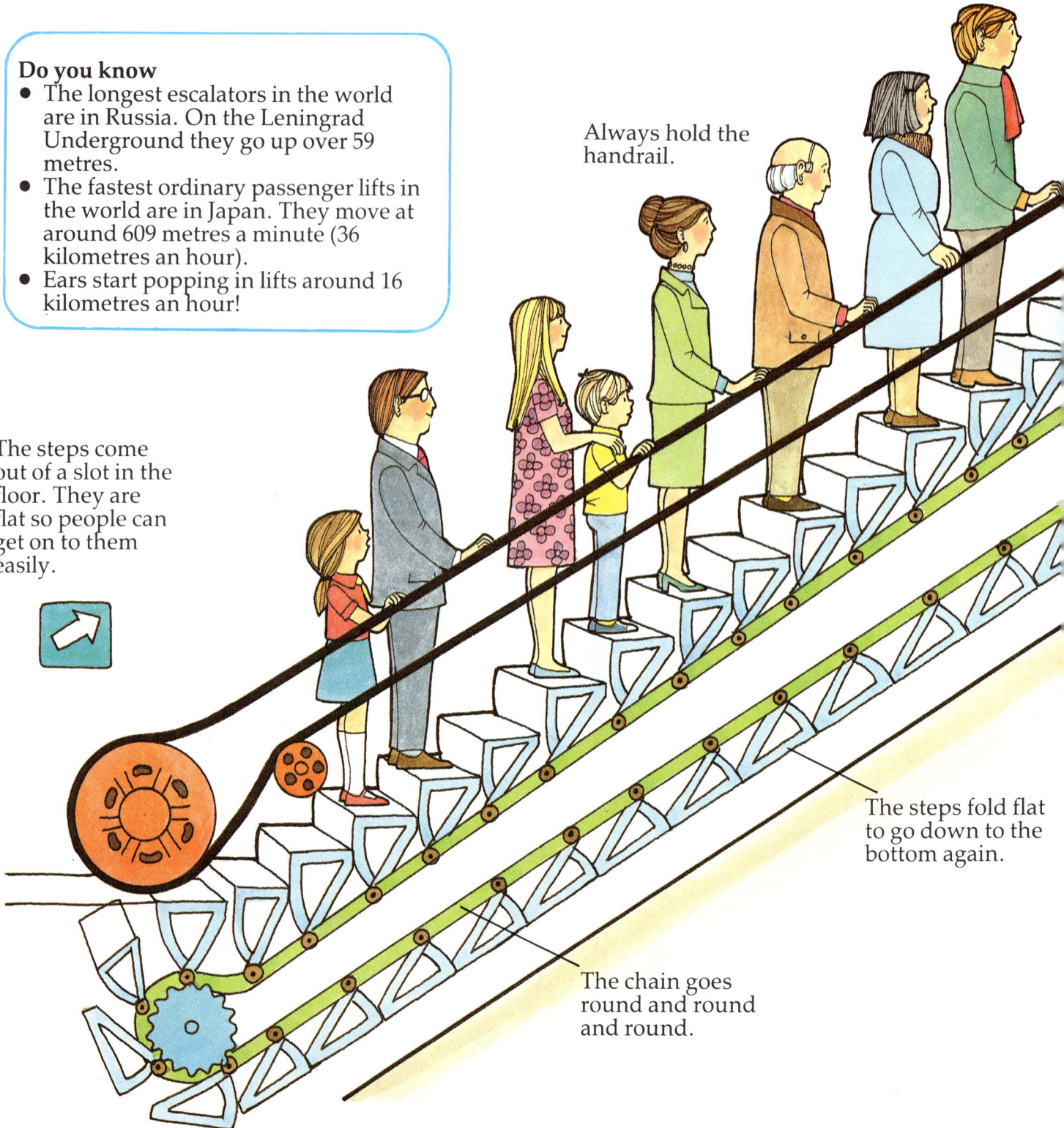

# A Lift

Lifts carry people up and down. The lift car is balanced by a heavy counterweight. When the counterweight goes down, the lift goes up. When the counterweight goes up, the lift goes down.

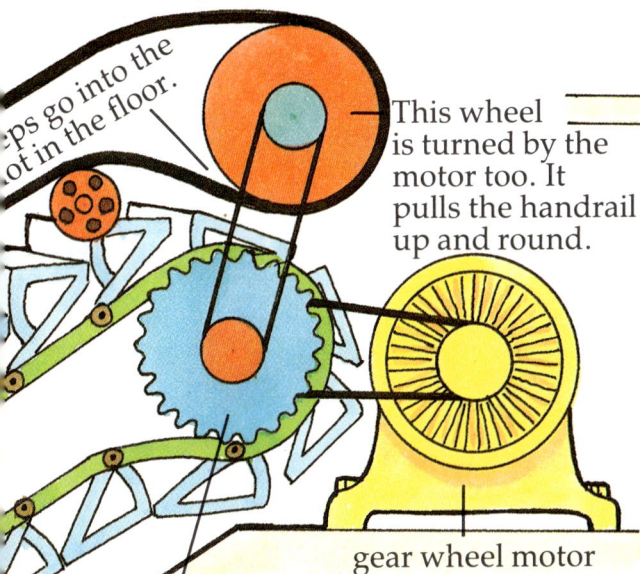

...ps go into the ...ot in the floor.

This wheel is turned by the motor too. It pulls the handrail up and round.

gear wheel motor

This wheel has teeth. The teeth fit into the chain and help pull the steps round.

The electric motor turns a wheel. The wheel has teeth. It pulls the chain and the steps on the chain come up.

**See how a lift works**
Tie two things about the same weight to a long piece of string. Wind the middle of the string round a short strong stick. Wind the string up round the stick one way, and watch one car come up like a lift. Wind it the other way, and the other car will come up like a counterweight while the 'lift' goes down.

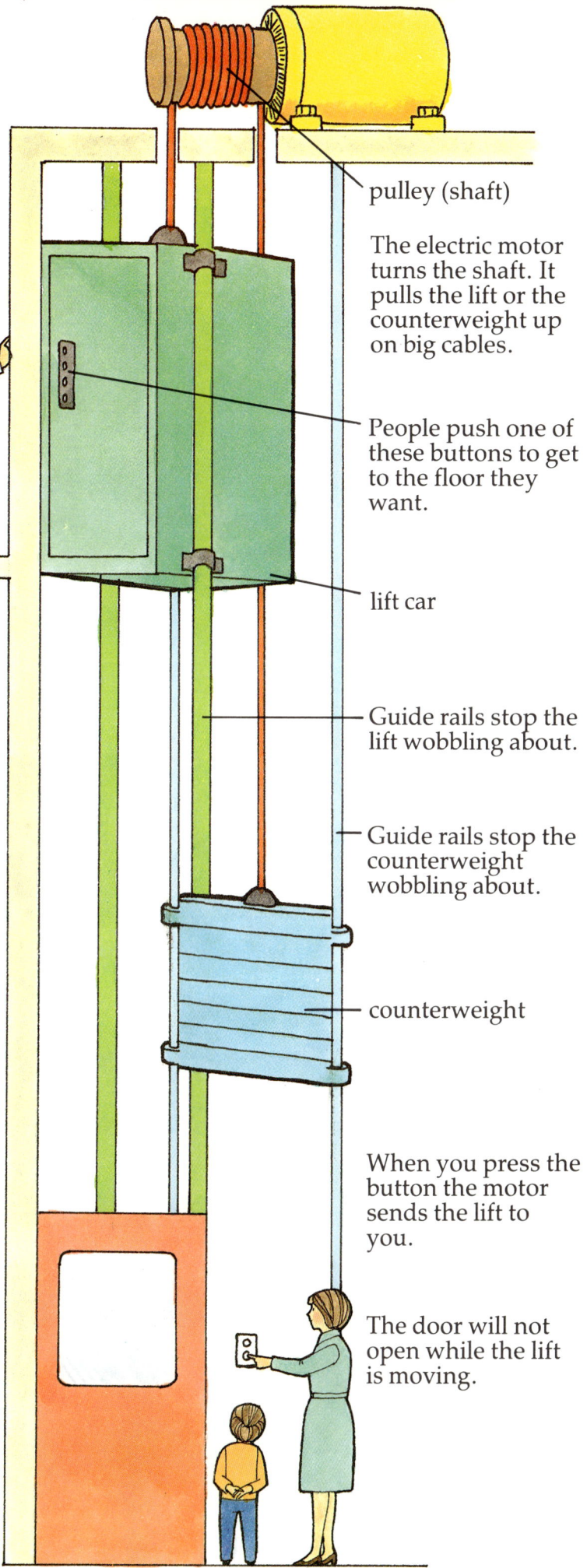

pulley (shaft)

The electric motor turns the shaft. It pulls the lift or the counterweight up on big cables.

People push one of these buttons to get to the floor they want.

lift car

Guide rails stop the lift wobbling about.

Guide rails stop the counterweight wobbling about.

counterweight

When you press the button the motor sends the lift to you.

The door will not open while the lift is moving.

# A Car

To start a car, the driver turns the ignition key on the dashboard and electricity runs from the battery to turn the starting motor.

1 Petrol goes from the fuel tank to the fuel pump.

2 The fuel pump sends petrol to the carburettor.

3 This sends a mix of petrol and air to the cylinders.

8 The driveshaft turns the rear axle.

7 The crankshaft turns the driveshaft.

6 The pistons turn the crankshaft.

9 The axle turns the wheels – and so makes the car go.

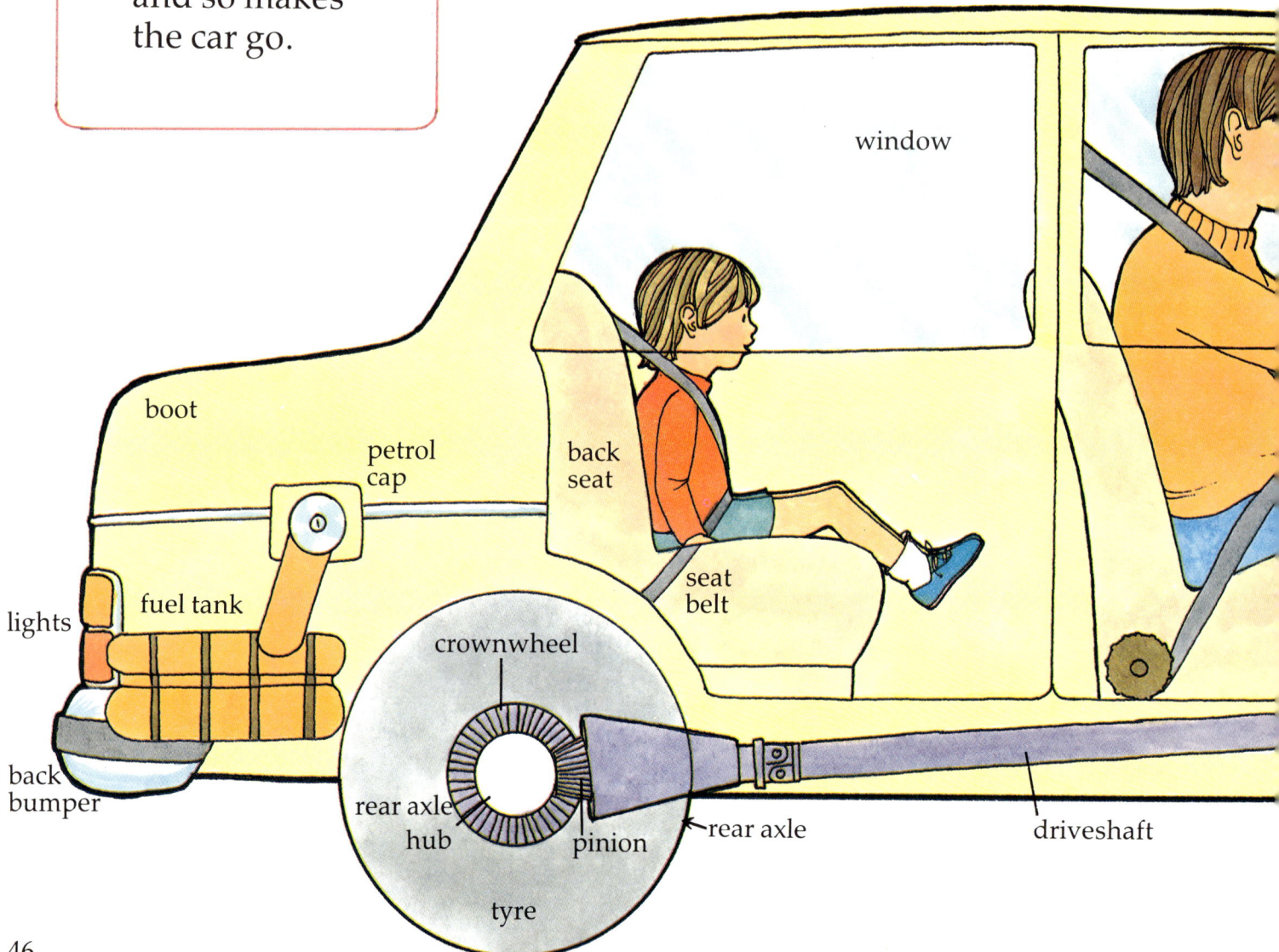

window

boot

petrol cap

back seat

lights

fuel tank

seat belt

crownwheel

back bumper

rear axle hub

pinion

rear axle

driveshaft

tyre

**The dashboard**

rear view mirror

steering wheel

wiper    milometer

speedometer

temperature gauge

fuel gauge

indicator    ignition

dashboard

clutch    brake

accelerator

The clutch pedal takes the crankshaft away from the gears, so that the gear lever can move the gears.

4 The sparking plug sets fire to the mixture.

5 Heat makes the cylinder pistons go up and down.

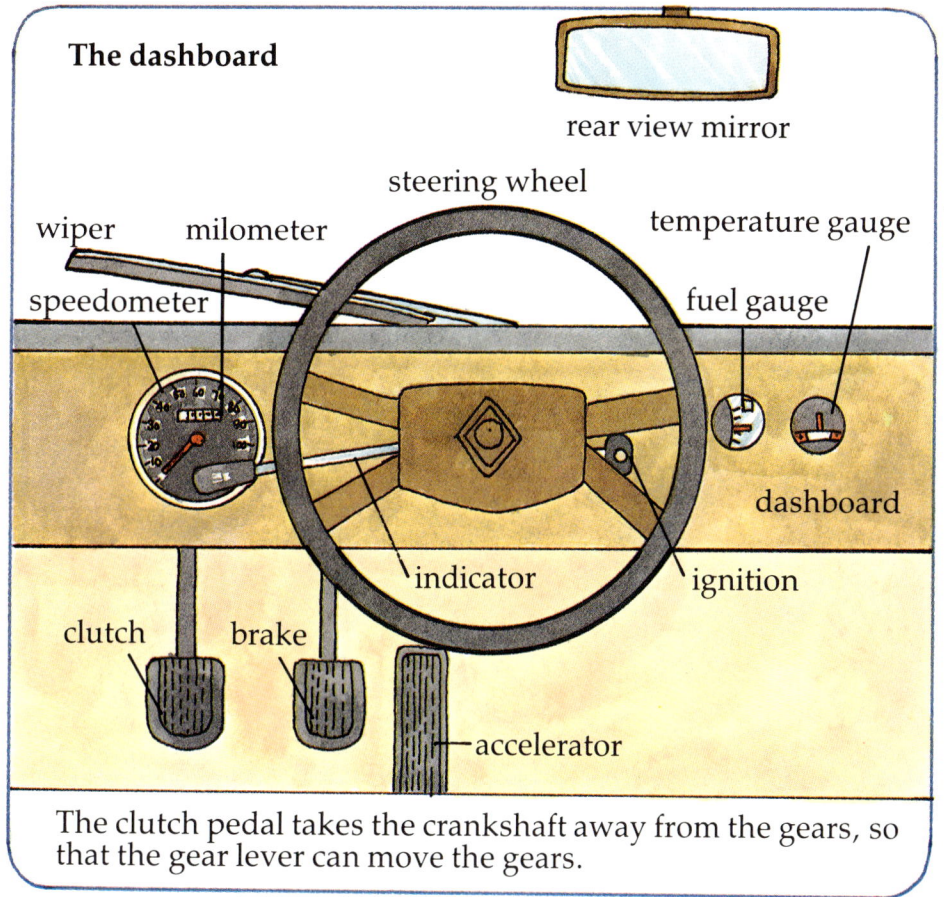

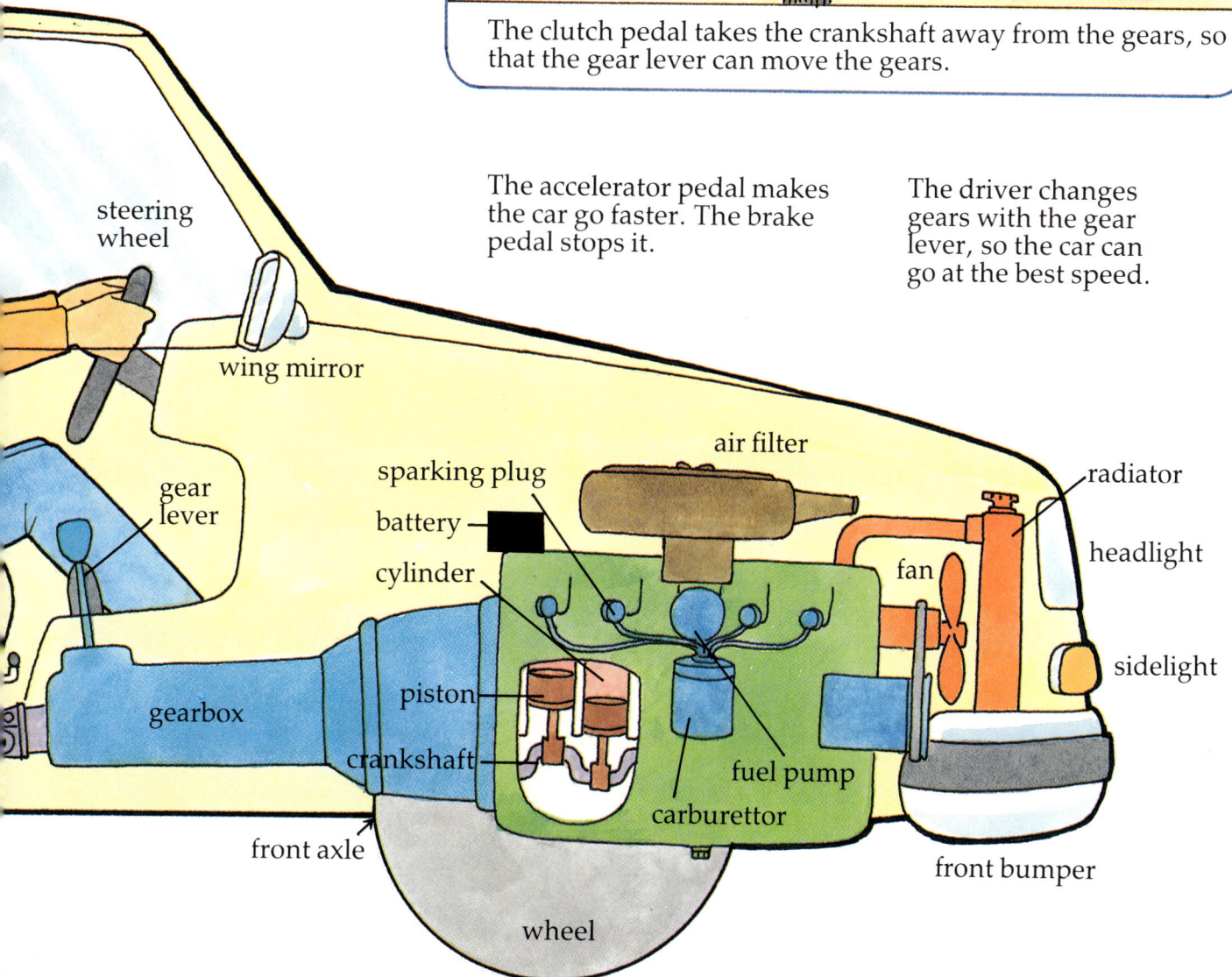

The accelerator pedal makes the car go faster. The brake pedal stops it.

The driver changes gears with the gear lever, so the car can go at the best speed.

steering wheel

wing mirror

gear lever

gearbox

sparking plug

battery

cylinder

piston

crankshaft

front axle

wheel

air filter

radiator

headlight

fan

sidelight

fuel pump

carburettor

front bumper

# A Fire Engine

When people are in danger, they need to be rescued quickly. A fire engine must get to a fire as fast as possible. An ambulance must get to an accident and a police car must hurry to the scene of a crime.

Fire engines, police cars and ambulances sound sirens or ring bells to tell people to get out of their way.

The fireman wears a special uniform with a helmet. He wears breathing apparatus to go into smoky buildings.

tool box

buckets

ladders

rope box

first aid box

hoses

crowbars

shovels

axes

hose

There is all sorts of equipment in the fire engine.

blankets

tool boxes

The fireman's axe helps him break down locked doors.

The hoses are for water or foam to put out the fire.

The siren makes a loud noise.

Ladders help firemen rescue people from tall buildings.

There are lots of other tools and first aid equipment in the side and back of the engine.

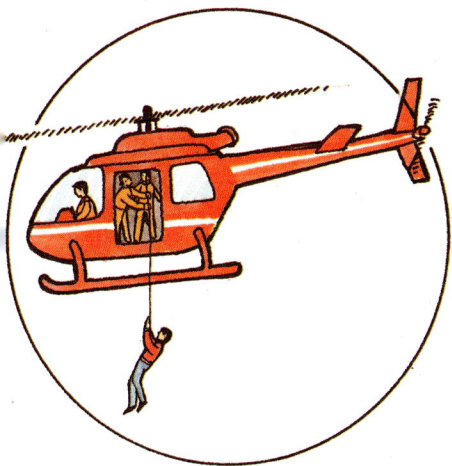

**Air-sea rescue**
Helicopters rescue people from the water when the sea is too rough for lifeboats.

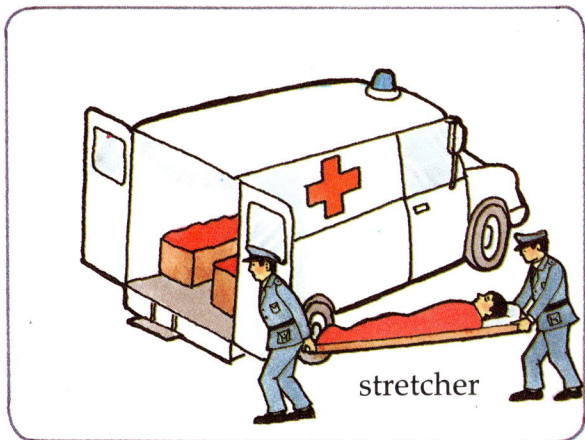

stretcher

flashing lights

breathing apparatus

driver

**Ambulance**
Inside an ambulance there are two beds, oxygen for breathing and all kinds of first aid equipment. Ambulance men are trained to save people's lives.

**Police car**
Police cars have radios to keep in touch with the police station. In the boot there are cones, lights and emergency traffic signs.

POLICE

cones

# A Combine Harvester

Long ago people all cut wheat by hand. Today a big combine harvester can cut it instead. The combine also picks up the wheat, separates the ears from the stalks, and can tie the stalks into bales.

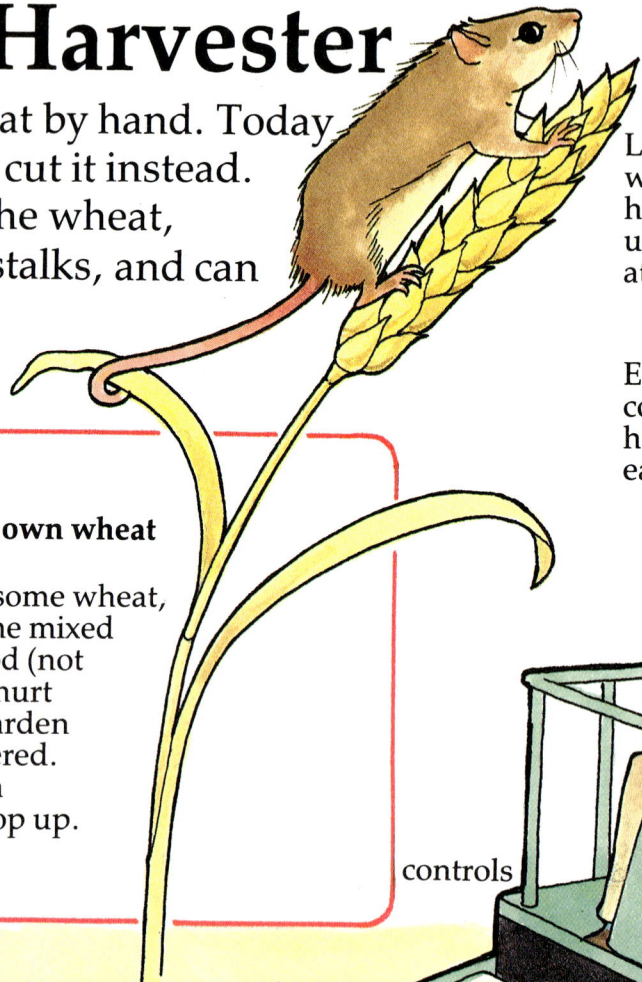

Little mice that live in wheatfields are called harvest mice. You usually only see them at harvest time.

Ear baffles stop the combine's noise hurting the driver's ears.

**Grow your own wheat**

To grow some wheat, plant some mixed rabbit food (not pellets) in a yoghurt pot or in your garden and keep it watered. All sorts of grain plants should pop up.

driver

controls

pick-up reel

auger

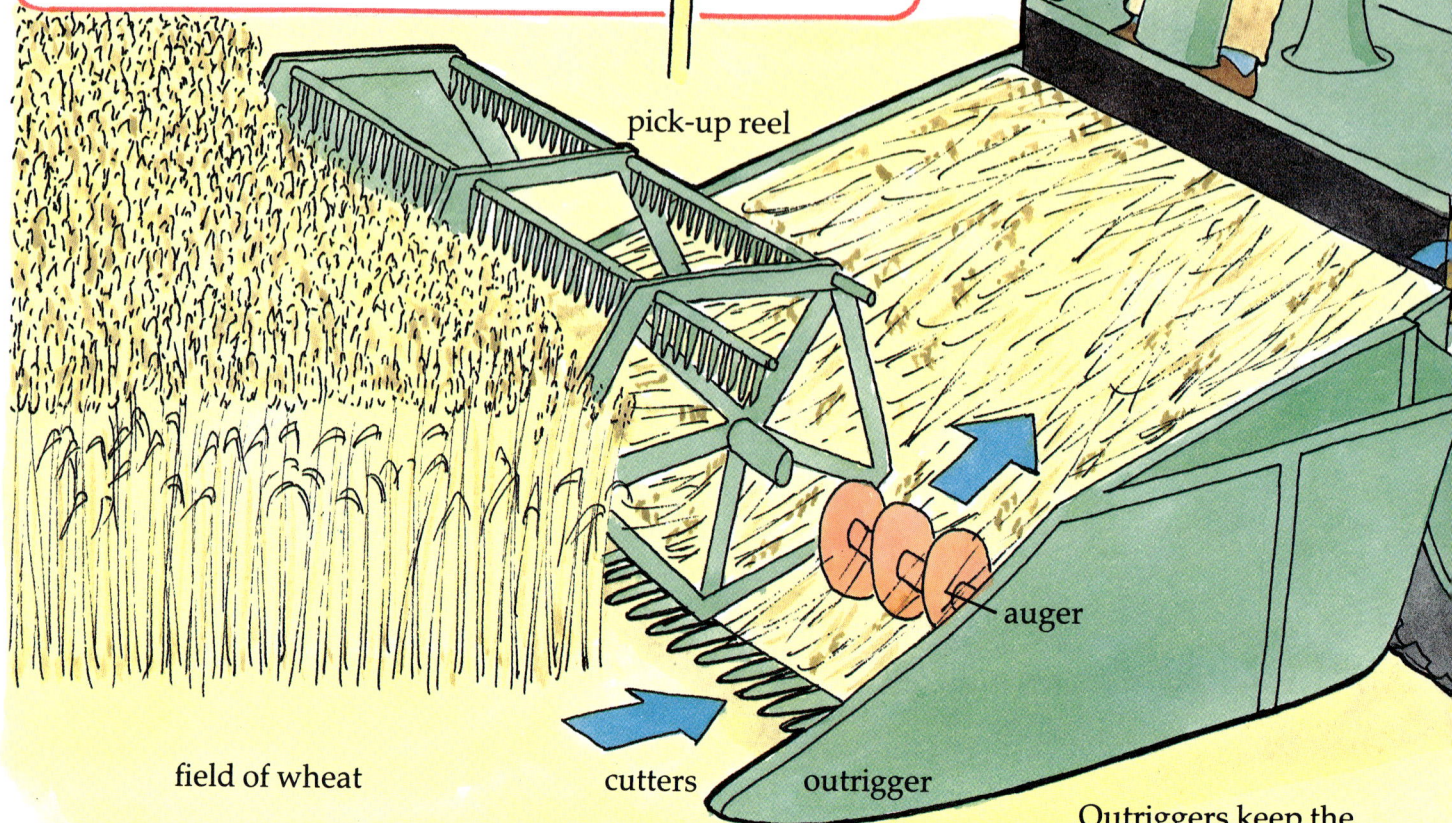

field of wheat

cutters

outrigger

Outriggers keep the combine steady.

1 The pick-up reel has whirling blades. They pull the wheat on to the cutters.

2 The auger pulls the cut wheat on to the conveyor.

3 The thresher pulls the ears off the stalks.

4 The conveyor takes the ears to the storage tank.

5 The shaker jiggles off the chaff. The chaff then blows away.

6 The stalks are baled. The bales fall to the ground.

7 The funnel pours out a stream of ears (grain) into a tractor, which takes the grain away.

8 The ears of wheat are ground into flour for bread, cakes and biscuits. The outside of the ear (called chaff) is not used. The stalk is used for straw.

storage tank

funnel

bale

The spyhole shows the driver how much wheat is in the tank.

baler

esher

shaker

conveyor

motor

tractor

# A Train

This is an electric train. Electric trains run on electricity from overhead wires or a third rail.

restaurant

carriage

carriage

carriage

wheels

**A steam train**
Steam trains use steam to push pistons which drive the wheels.

**A diesel train**
Diesel trains have cylinders and pistons like cars. They run on diesel fuel.

buffet car      carriage      guard's van

coupling

The transformer changes the electricity to the right voltage.

The pantograph arm collects electricity from the wire.

overhead electric wire

cab 2

cooling air louvres

signals

cab 1

The traction motor turns the wheels.

41

lights

buffers

batteries for light and heat

rails

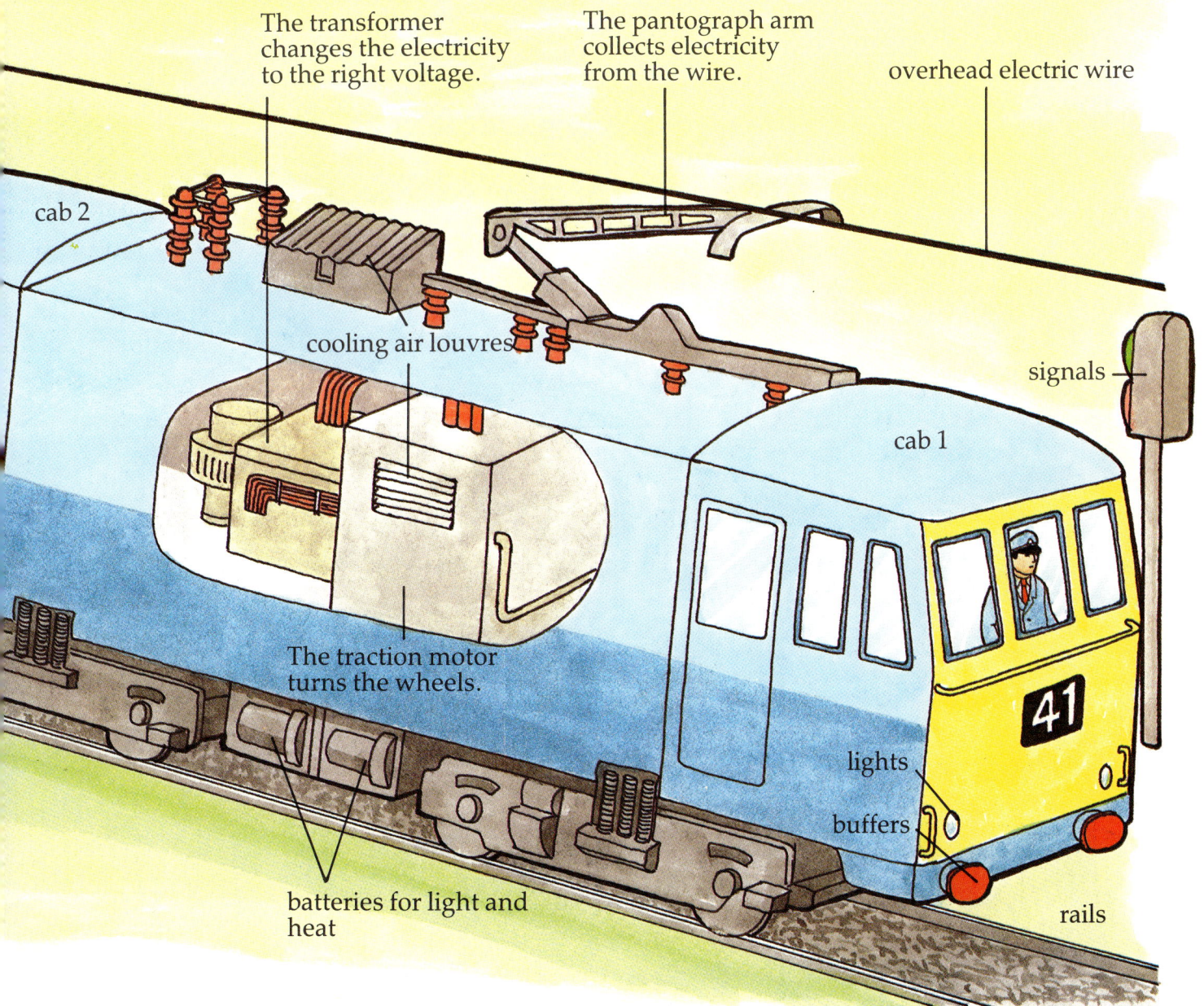

# A Ship

This big ship carries people and cargo round the world.
She is like a floating hotel.
She carries everything her passengers need.

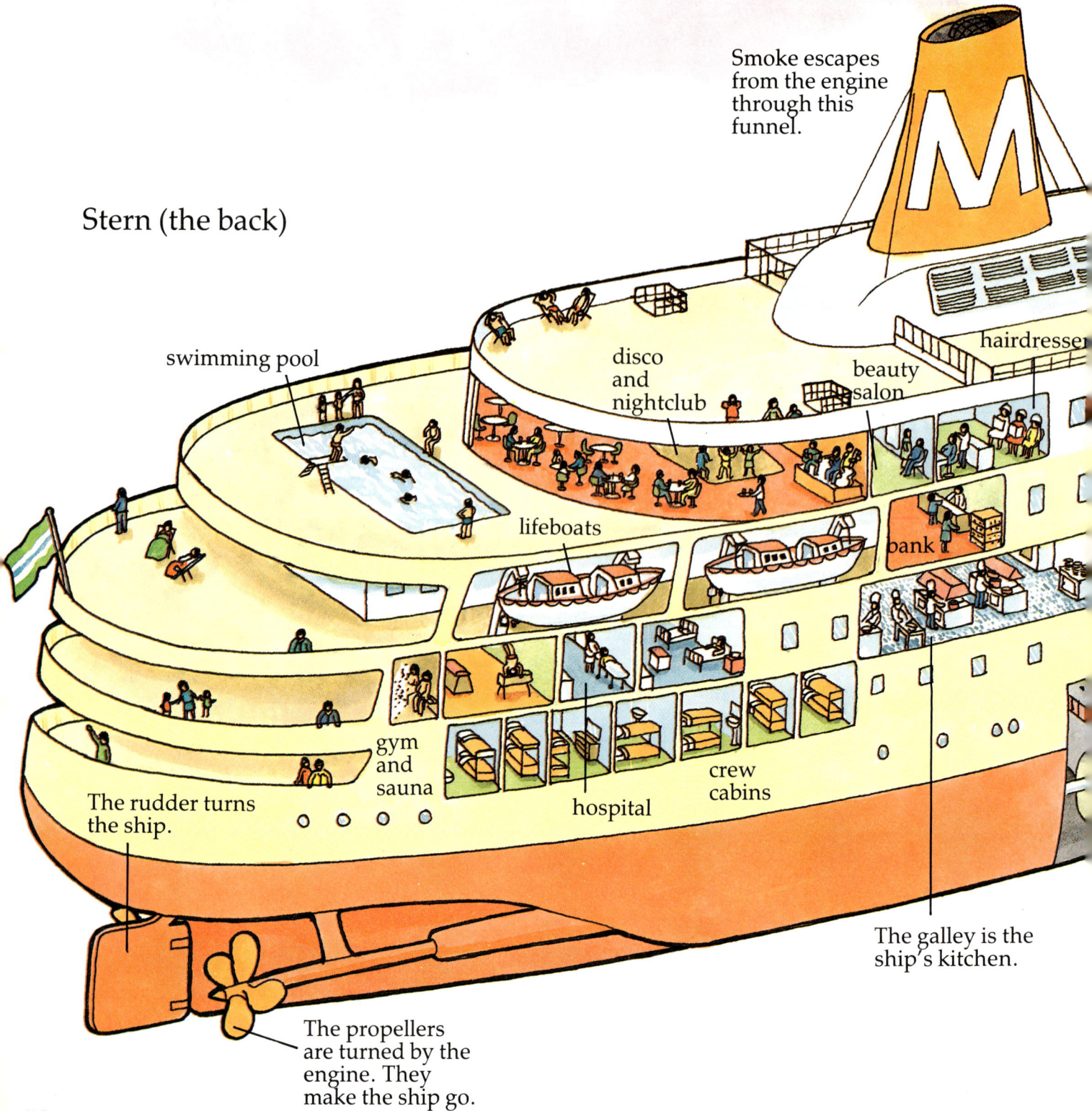

Smoke escapes from the engine through this funnel.

Stern (the back)

swimming pool

disco and nightclub

beauty salon

hairdresser

lifeboats

bank

gym and sauna

hospital

crew cabins

The rudder turns the ship.

The galley is the ship's kitchen.

The propellers are turned by the engine. They make the ship go.

The look-out watches high up in the crow's nest

The helmsman turns the wheel to steer the ship.

The crane moves cargo from shore to ship.

radio room

mast

bridge

chartroom

captain

children's playroom

shops

bar

anchor

library

lounge

passenger cabins

garage

plimsoll line (when the ship is full of cargo, this line is level with the water)

dining room

cinema

cargo hold

The stabilizers keep the ship from rolling too much from side to side.

engine

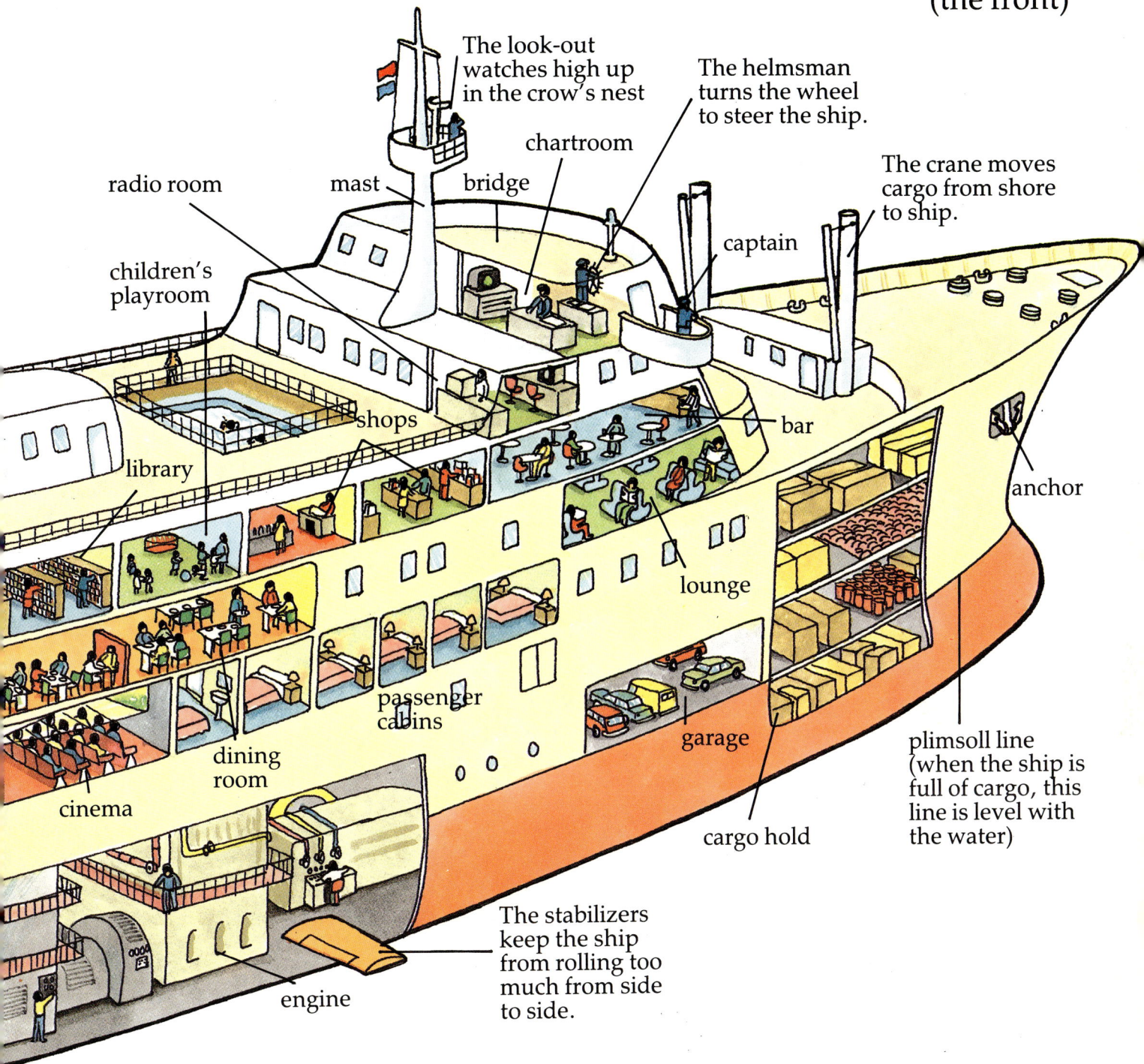

The main body of a ship is called the hull. On top of the hull and inside it there are several layers called decks.

This ship has a sports deck on top, with the captain's bridge at one end. Below it are the promenade deck, two cabin decks and a garage deck.

In the bottom of the hull there are tanks of fuel oil and the engine room, where huge noisy motors turn the propeller shaft to make the ship go.

# The Space Shuttle

The space shuttle takes off like a rocket. It travels through space like a spacecraft and lands like an aeroplane. It can be used over and over again to carry men and all sorts of useful machines into space. It can stay in space for a week.

**Spacelab**
This is a laboratory full of scientific equipment for doing experiments in space.

**Cargo bay**
The cargo bay holds telescopes and satellites to be launched into orbit.

When the shuttle is in orbit, the cargo bay doors open.

main rocket engines

The outside is covered by protective tiles.

**Cockpit**
The pilots and the passengers sit here during take-off and landing. The shuttle is launched by a rocket which drops back to Earth.

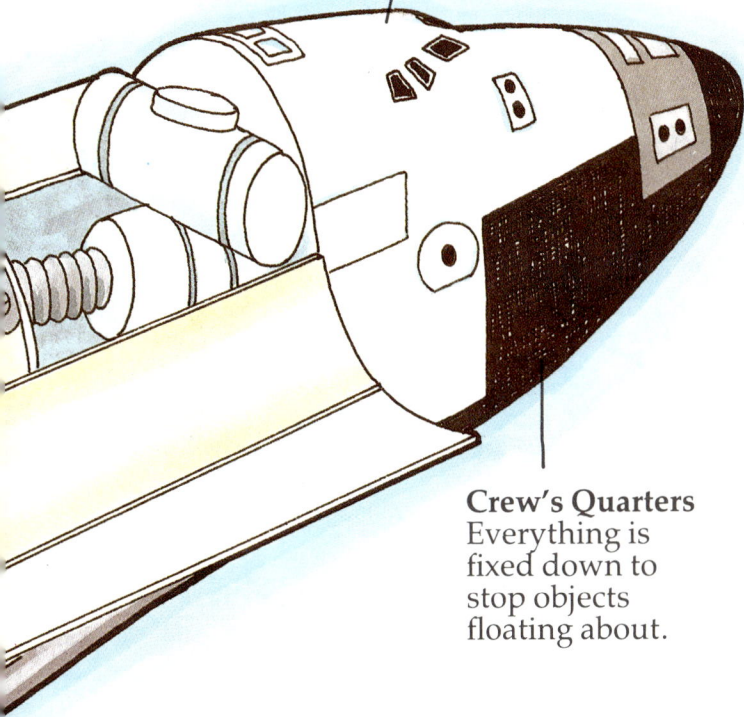

The crew eat and work at a table like this. They slip their feet into straps on the floor.

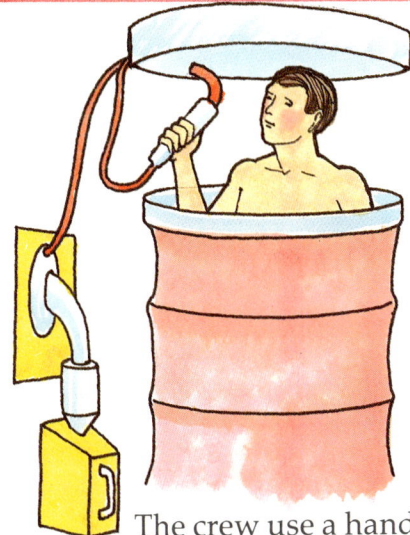

**Crew's Quarters**
Everything is fixed down to stop objects floating about.

There is no gravity in space, so everything is weightless, even the crew. They float about the cabin and if they 'drop' something, it just floats away.

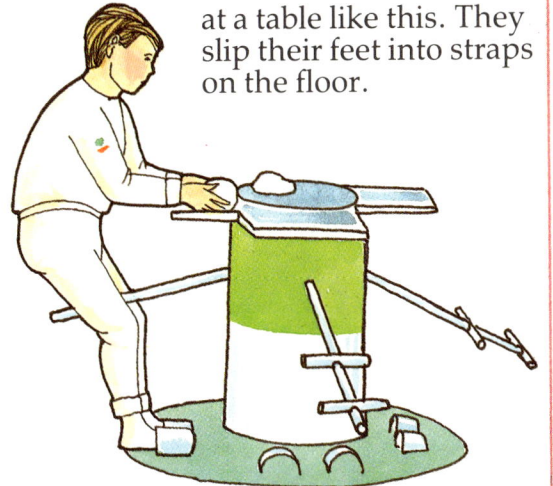

The crew use a hand spray to shower. They close the lid of the tub to stop water flying about.

There is no point lying down to sleep if you are weightless. The crew go to sleep in sleeping bags hung from the wall.

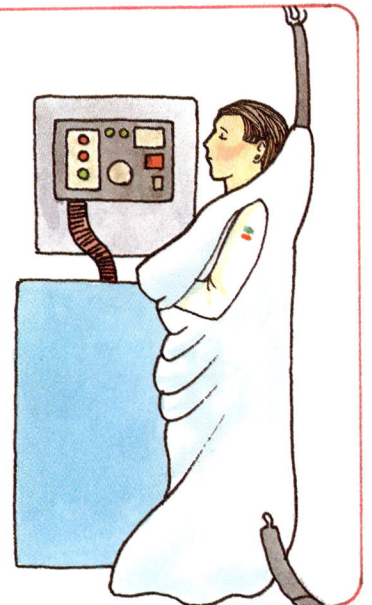

# What Do You Know?

**Match the pairs**

Find the answers on page 62

combine    harvester

apple

cocoa pod

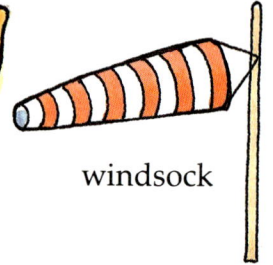
windsock

bird

butterfly

bee

TV camera

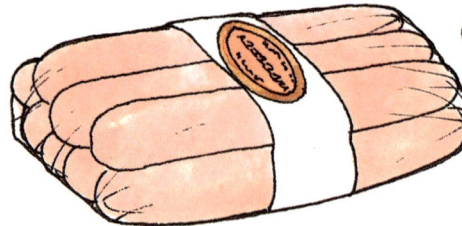
sausages

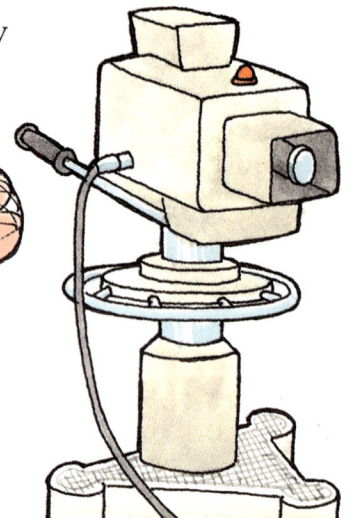

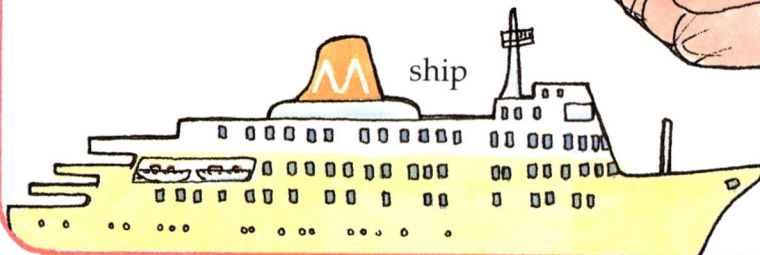
ship

**Do you remember?**

1 Which animal nests in tree roots? (page 8)
2 What kind of watch shows the time in numbers? (page 25)
3 What was a motte? (page 42)
4 Which animals keep greenfly as 'cows'? (page 10)
5 What does an agitator do? (page 31)

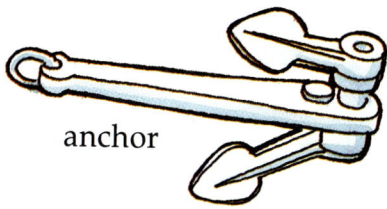
anchor

wheat

TV set

hive

aeroplane

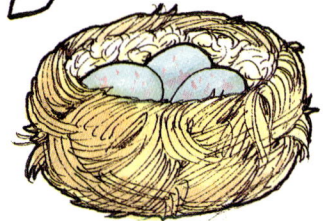
nest

shopping trolley

tree

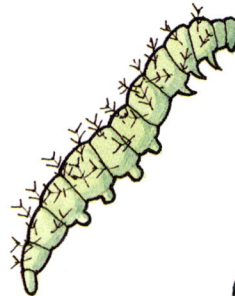
caterpillar

bar of chocolate

6  What does an electric till do? (page 35)

7  What is concrete made from? (page 36)

8  Which strings make low notes – long or short? (page 23)

9  Where are the longest escalators in the world? (page 44)

10  What does the accelerator do? (page 47)

If you need a clue, look at the page numbered in brackets.
Check your answers on page 62.

# More Puzzles

**What's its name?**

1 (page 16)

2 (page 23)

3 (page 43)

4 (page 40)

5 (page 25)

6 (page 31)

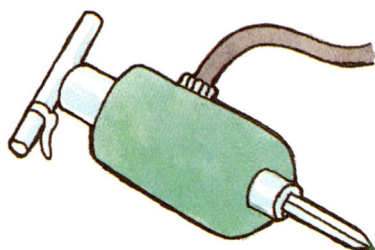

7 (page 36)

8 (page 31)

9 (page 12)

10 (page 28)

Look for clues on the pages numbered in brackets

# Which turns into which?

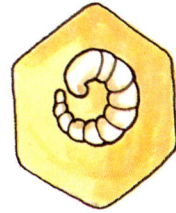

Look up 'Ant', 'Bee' and 'Butterfly' in the index to find where you can check your answers.

# What animals are these?

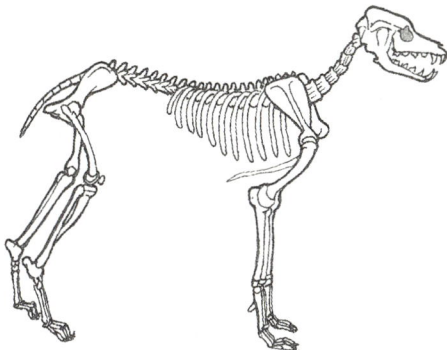

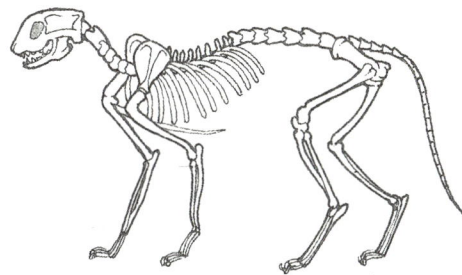

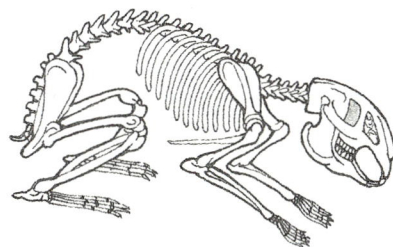

You can check your answers on page 21.

# Answers

**Page 58**    **Match the pairs**

apple: tree
cocoa pod: bar of chocolate
windsock: aeroplane
combine harvester: wheat
bird: nest
butterfly: caterpillar
bee: hive
ship: anchor
sausages: shopping trolley
TV camera: TV set

**Page 58**    **Do you remember?**

1 Woodmouse
2 Digital watch
3 A small hill with a castle on it
4 Ants
5 Spins the tub in a washing machine
6 Adds up the prices
7 Sand, cement, stones and water
8 Long
9 Leningrad, Russia
10 Makes the car go faster

**Page 60**    **What's its name?**

1 Chrysalis
2 Piano
3 Arrow slit
4 Nose wheel truck
5 Cuckoo clock
6 Juice squeezer
7 Pneumatic drill
8 Vacuum cleaner
9 Queen bee
10 Microphone

# Index

**Things to do**